KU-478-399

QUEENPIN

A young woman hired to keep the books at a down-at-heel nightclub is taken under the wing of the infamous Gloria Denton, a mob luminary who reigned during the Golden Era of Bugsy Siegel and Lucky Luciano. The moll to end all molls, Gloria is notoriously cunning and ruthless. She shows her eager young protégée the ropes, ushering her into a glittering whirl of late-night casinos, racetracks, and big, big money, but it all falls to pieces with a few turns of the roulette wheel, as both mentor and protégée scramble to stay one step ahead of their bosses and each other.

QUEENPIN

QUEENPIN

by

Megan Abbott

Magna Large Print Books
Long Preston, North Yorkshire,
BD23 4ND, England.

British Library Cataloguing in Publication Data.

Abbott, Megan
    Queenpin.

    A catalogue record of this book is
    available from the British Library

    ISBN   978-0-7505-3290-7

First published in Great Britain by Pocket Books UK, 2009
An imprint of Simon & Schuster UK Ltd.

Copyright © 2007 by Megan Abbott

Cover illustration © Richie Fateyl by arrangement with
Chris Nurse

The right of Megan Abbott to be identified as the author of this
work has been asserted in accordance with sections 77 and 78 of
the Copyright, Designs and Patents Act, 1988

Published in Large Print 2010 by arrangement with
Simon & Schuster UK Ltd.

All Rights reserved. No part of this publication may be
reproduced, stored in a retrieval system, or transmitted in any
form or by any means, electronic, mechanical, photocopying,
recording or otherwise without the prior permission of the
Copyright owner.

Magna Large Print is an imprint of Library Magna Books Ltd.

Printed and bound in Great Britain by
T.J. (International) Ltd., Cornwall, PL28 8RW

This book is a work of fiction.
Names, characters, places and incidents
are either a product of the author's
imagination or are used fictitiously.
Any resemblance to actual people,
living or dead, events or locales,
is entirely coincidental.

For Josh,
a lanky brunette with a wicked jaw

ACKNOWLEDGEMENTS

Deeply felt thanks to the incomparable Denise Roy, without whom. My continuing gratitude to the dauntless Paul Cirone and the Friedrich Agency. Also, for their role in the origin of this lurid tale: Allan Guthrie, Duane Swierczynski, David Thompson, and McKenna Jordan.

With love beyond measure to Kiki and her darling Brody. Special thanks and love to Philip & Patricia Abbott, Joshua Abbott, Julie Nichols, Alison Levy, Darcy Lockman, Ralph & Janet Nase, Jeff, Ruth & Stephen Nase, Dee Maloney and the entire, big-hearted Gaylord family from coast to coast.

I want the legs.

That was the first thing that came into my head. The legs were the legs of a twenty-year-old Vegas showgirl, a hundred feet long and with just enough curve and give and promise. Sure, there was no hiding the slightly worn hands or the beginning tugs of skin framing the bones in her face. But the legs, they lasted, I tell you. They endured. Two decades her junior, my skinny matchsticks were no competition.

In the casinos, she could pass for thirty. The low lighting, her glossy auburn hair, legs swinging, tapping the bottom rim of the tall bettor stools. At the track, though, she looked her age. Even swathed in oversized sunglasses, a wide-brimmed hat, bright gloves, she couldn't outflank the merciless sunshine, the glare off the grandstand. Not that it mattered. She was legend.

I was never sure what she saw in me. *You looked like you knew a thing or two*, she told me later. *But were ready to learn a lot more.*

It was a soft sell, a long sell. I never knew what she had in mind until I already had

13

such a taste I thought my tongue would never stop buzzing. Meaning, she got me in, she got me jobs, she got me fat stacks of cash too thick to wedge down my cleavage. She got me in with the hard boys, the fast money, and I couldn't get enough. I wanted more. *Give me more.*

When I met her, I was doing the books at Club Tee Hee, a rinky-dink joint on the east side, one of a twinkling row of red- and blue-lit joints the cops never touched. Starlite Strip, it was called, optimistically.

I'd been working there a few months. Accounts paid and receivable. Payroll. My old man knew the owners, red-eyed, slump-shouldered Jerome and his terrier-faced brother-in-law, Arthur. Had filled their vending machines – cigarettes for the front hallway, perfume and face powders for the ladies' room, men's stuff for the men's room – for fifteen years. And they liked the old man, had a funny kind of respect for his churchgoing, working-stiff life – widower, paid his bills, three daughters, all of whom reached age twenty without a stint at Agnes Millan's Home for Wayward Girls. My old man, he didn't like the idea of sending me to work at a nightclub, but he did like the idea of me having a job sitting at a desk over rows of numbers rather than my last gig, which was modeling dresses for leering business-men at Hickey's Department Store, where the pay is cut-rate unless you went off the books and to hotel suites for private parties. I never went to one of those parties, but let's be honest, it was only a matter of time.

'With that figure and that puss,' Jerome said, 'you can't blame him for wanting to keep you buried in a back office, behind a green visor, sugar cake.' Jerome and Arthur came off as decent men, given their trade, profiting from the sinning ways of hopeless souls. Pop knew firsthand they always paid their vending bills and went home each night to thick-ankled wives and a couple of kids, had lived in the same modest houses in the Sycamore district as long as anyone could remember. So he figured them for honest joes. And he was wrong. My old man never was too bright, never saw the angles. That's how you end up never making two dimes in vending, one of the crookedest rackets there is. I loved the guy, but I knew a week in that the Tee Hee was bought and paid for five times over by the city big boys and Jerome and Arthur were in over their heads.

The job was easy. Mornings, I took advanced accounting at the Dolores Grey Business School. Afternoons, I took the city bus to the Tee Hee. I tallied time sheets, paid the liquor bills, supply invoices, rent, and insurance. And I looked the part, decked out in my Orlon sweater, tweed skirt, one-inch heels, round toes, my unpolished nails pressing the adding machine keys, counting the whiskey-stained dollar bills. But I never believed in it.

Hell, I'll admit it, I had a taste for the other from the start. Where would a twenty-two-year-old kid rather be? Setting the table for a corned beef and cabbage dinner with her old man, forks scraping, moths fluttering against the window, the briny smell from the kitchen sinking into my skin with each tock of the imitation grandfather clock? Or gliding my way through the fuzzy dark of the Tee Hee, vibrating with low, slow jazz, clusters of juniper-breathed men and women touching, hands on lapels, fingers on silk nylons, cigarettes releasing willowy clouds into every acid green banquette? Sure, it was no El Morocco, but in this town, it might as well have been. The place felt alive, I could hear it beating in my chest, between my hips, everywhere. Clock-out time and I never wanted to leave. I'd grin my way into a Tom

16

Collins from Shep, the lantern-jawed bartender, and watch from the corner stool, watch everything, eating green cherries, the candied drink soaking into my lips, my tongue.

There were about three hours of actual work for every seven hours on the clock. That's how I figured there would be different duties on the horizon, if I passed the test, whatever the test would be. And it started soon enough.

It was all so easy. With or without Dolores Grey Business School, I could make those digits fall in line and when Jerome asked me to cook the books, I did it.

'Muffin, there's this new way of doing things I'd like to try,' he said, leaning over me at my desk, stubby finger on my ledger.

'Sure, Mr. Bendix. I can do that,' I said, looking him in the eye. I wanted him to see that I was no fool. That I got the game – and believe me, anyone would have gotten the game – and was still up for it. Looking back, I don't know why I wasn't more scared of getting pinched or worse. But it never really ran that way for me. I saw a chance, I took it. I didn't want to miss my ticket.

The method Jerome had in mind was so

creaky you'd have thought it went out with detachable collars and petticoats. It was like asking to be caught. But he didn't seem to be breaking a sweat about it. So I figured he'd gotten orders on this and felt protected. The Tee Hee was under an umbrella and the boys felt safe and dry. For a time, at least.

I'd been working the new system four of five days when I first saw her. The place was hissing with stories told behind hands as she walked into the place. About the big gees and button men she'd tossed with back in the day, everyone from Dutch Schultz to Joey Adonis and Lucky himself.

Turns out, she came every few weeks, sipping a club soda with a twist and counting Jerome's vig before she drove off in her alpine white El Dorado to kick it Upstairs. Her name was Gloria Denton.

Jerome, Arthur, the regulars, they loved to talk about her, share stories, tales, legends. About how, in the glory days, she used to carry a long-handled pair of scissors in her purse when she collected in the rough parts of town, about the time an angry wife tried to run her over with her Cadillac outside her husband's betting parlor, about a stripper named Candy Annie who crossed her on some deal back in '48 but, when Annie walked into the ladies' room at the Breakwater Hotel in Miami three months later, Gloria got her revenge with a straight-edge razor, gutting the stripper like a fish.

'Who is she anyhow?' I asked, that first time. 'Whose wife?'

'She's no one's wife,' Jerome said, shaking his head. 'And she's no moll, never was, not even when she was fresh and tight as Kim Novak.'

'What's she, some kind of kingpin?'

Jerome shook his head. 'Not like that. She's on the inside. She's one of them. They trust her. She's been around forever. In her heyday, she ran with the real pros, back when they owned the whole show, their own national wire service, not just little numbers rigs in sunken-in burgs like this one. She and Virginia Hill, they were the two gals that mattered past what they could pull in the sack.'

Soon enough I saw her eyeing me. Arthur said she'd been asking about me, where I came from. 'Who's the lollypop,' she asked. 'What's her story?' Later, I figured she must've heard about the way I could work things, work things and keep my mouth shut about it. She knew everybody and everybody knew her and she plucked me out of that two-bit hootchy-kootch and put me on the big stage, footlights up my dress.

I wanted more.

So when Jerome stepped it up, asked me to make him a fake numbers book for his single-action game, I did that too. I was a fast learner for a kid who never heard of running numbers, except in the pictures. I guessed it was a pretty chancy thing. What made guys like Jerome and Arthur, who couldn't stop the bartenders from padding tabs and pocketing the difference, think they could pull something over on the big-time boys who owned them wholesale, from their wispy forelocks to their cheap shoes?

It was ledge-crawling for the slickest of operators, writing a numbers book. But for schmoes like Jerome and Arthur it read like suicide. If I'd been around the rackets longer, I'd have told them to find another patsy. I was about to put myself on the chopping block but was too raw to know it. Too stupid to be scared.

The idea was to skip over the actual gathering-of-bets-from-customers part and instead dummy up a set of books with num-

bers Jerome and Arthur would play themselves. Then, when they hit, they'd get to
keep all the honey.

'You got the cash for it?' I asked. 'Even if
the bets are phony, you still gotta pass the
bag to Gloria Denton, like if you really were
collecting them.'

'Tell her, Jer,' Arthur sniffed anxiously,
pinching his nose like he did when he saw
Shep serving to jailbait. 'Tell her what you
conjured.'

Jerome smiled broadly. 'Week by week,
little girl. As long as luck holds, we'd score
winnings first part of the week to pass over
to Gloria at week's end. And this joint leaks
enough scratch to hold us over when the
lady Fortune ain't in our corner.'

'You don't think they're wise to this kind
of game? They've been in it a long time.'

'Since before you were a gleam in your
poppa's eye,' Jerome said, straightening his
cuffs. 'But they got bigger fish to fry. They're
not gonna notice one set of phony ribbons
in that leaning tower Gloria packs into her
tired trunk twice a month.'

'You're the boss.'

We'd been running it less than a week when
it took a bad turn. Mugs, the kid with the

ducktail who was our usual runner, didn't show up to take our betting slips and instead she was there, like an IRS auditor for the rackets. It was the first time she ever spoke to me.

I couldn't take my eyes off her. It was like a famous picture on the wall suddenly started yapping at you. I was staring, you bet. I wanted to take it all in, her whole setup. The half-moon manicured nails, pale green suit and hat, the pearl-ring brooch. Class. No gun moll, she.

It never crossed my mind that she'd start talking. When she did, I nearly jumped out of my swivel seat.

'Funny-looking book.'

'Yeah,' I said, trying not to fidget. 'Well, I haven't been doing it long. Looks pretty green, huh?'

'Just careful. Not the scratch sheet I usually see.'

She pulled a seven-column steno from her dyed-white alligator briefcase and set it in front of me. 'What do you notice?'

'Other than the coffee stains and the bad penmanship?' I said.

'Yes, other than that.' Straight face. Always a straight face.

I looked at it, squinting at the curled

pages. 'Different color inks. Different pens. Even a grease pencil here?'

'And different weights, angles. What do you make of it?'

'Bets were recorded at different times, in different places. Maybe standing here, sitting at a desk or counter here. With a racing form pencil here, so maybe scribbled down at a betting parlor.'

She ran her hand over my book, with its tidy columns, its uniform blue figures in crisp Dolores Grey script. She didn't say anything. She didn't need to. In my head, I cursed Jerome and Arthur for not telling me how ribbons should look, how, at least at places like the Tee Hee, they're filled over time, not all at once, at a desk. Schmucks. Slapping big fat targets on all of us.

'So where'd all these new bets come from?' she asked. 'First time I ever saw two books at the Tee Hee.'

'Kilapsky Brothers Vending Machine employees,' I said. That was the nursery rhyme Jerome told me to recite if asked. 'They're new and so am I, so Jerome and Arthur put me in charge of doing ribbons for them.'

'They cut you in?'

'Should they?'

She looked at me. 'Must be a reason to have a whole separate book,' she said.

'They wanted to see how I made out first. They didn't want me fouling their setup. So a separate book to keep track.'

'So these Kilapsky boys never had any action until you came along?'

'Not that I know of. They're family men. Spend their Friday nights at the VFW.'

'You know who owns Kilapsky?'

'The brothers. Junior is the head guy now,' I said.

'That so?' she said and that's when I got it. Her bosses really owned Kilapsky and I was the schmuck. They probably already had a controller taking bets from those employees. She'd been stringing me along from the minute we started talking, watching me dig my own grave. My only choice was to take it all the way and play the prize-one chump.

'That's what Jerome and Arthur told me,' I said. 'They pass me the slips each morning and I fill out the ribbon. It's duck soup, so who am I to complain?' Sure, it was kind of a rotten move to pitch it all on Jerome and Arthur. But they were rotten guys. Hell if I was going to hang for them. They'd've sold me up the river for a song, maybe already had.

24

She gave me a prisonyard stare and I thought I almost saw a smile crimp those crimson lips. 'Who are you to complain,' she repeated, tossing my steno back at me. 'Keep at it, ace. Keep at it.'

I didn't get it. But I would.

The next week I saw her again. She was walking across the Tee Hee parking lot, taking short steps in her fitted suit, her pointy-toe heels – snakeskin, I was sure. She was looking straight at me as I stood by the bus stop, shivering in my rayon coat, tapping my feet to keep warm.

'I'll drop you. Get in,' she said, nodding toward the El Dorado.

My pop had warned me about this kind of invitation, but only from jumpy-eyed or slick-faced men, salesmen and bar patrons, barmen and kitchen help, suppliers and deliverers, custodians and busboys. Never from anyone in spiky heels with a gold-clasped clutch of creamy leather under her arm and gold button earrings and a sharp green rock balancing on one long finger, a sleek charm bracelet swaying from one wrist, dangling like a promise.

Who was I to say no?

After all, the old man's rule book was

mum on taking lifts from middle-aged ladies.

I started toward her car.

My, did the leather seats feel fine. And the car warmed up so fast and had the rich smell of good cigarettes and department store perfume.

'Where to?' she said in a low voice as we made our way down the Starlite Strip.

'Pottsville section. On Fleetwood Way.'

She nodded, eyes on the road. 'Tough break, kid.'

I didn't know what she meant. At least not for sure.

'Must be a forty-minute bus ride home,' she continued, 'and all you get at the end is what? Vinyl siding and one picture window? Or is it a walk-up that takes you for a sleigh ride every time the commuter train heads eastbound or west?'

I sat up a little straighter and looked at her from the corner of my eye. 'Aluminum siding,' I murmured.

She didn't give me any I-told-you-so, no I-got-your-number. Instead, she said, 'Don't mistake me, kid. I grew up three kids to a bed on the south side of Coal City, USA. I'm just saying, time comes and you gotta crawl your way out.'

'I'm trying.'

'With those two chumps? Fat chance.' She shook her head wearily. 'Listen. Maybe you'd like some brighter opportunities.'

'A job?' I tried to keep a measured tone.

'Something like that, Dolly Dingle. Let's stop and I'll buy you a cup. I think it's time you put on your miner's hat and headed toward the bright light.'

For two hours we sat at the Triple R Diner on Eastern Boulevard and she did her thing. The slow-voiced, hard-eyed Mesmer routine I would come to know so well. All so logical, everything flowing like syrup off a spoon.

I've always known when to shut up and listen. Hands curled around my coffee cup, I said maybe five words. She was giving me the keys to the kingdom. I knew that much, even then. I just didn't know where the kingdom was. Truth was, I didn't care. I liked its shine even from a long distance.

She told me how her work afforded her a very comfortable lifestyle. It required significant discretion and considerable flexibility (she might, like a fireman or doctor, be called upon at a moment's notice to attend to duties). But in return there were substantial rewards. In material things, yes, and a way of living, but also with regard to the way one was treated, viewed. Still, there was a great deal of travel, long, late hours in the car or on trains, even airplanes. Now, after coming on twenty-five years, she could use a little help. And there was more than enough work to go around, for the right kind of girl. Smart, discreet, and with some fire in the belly.

Was that how she saw me?

Sure, I wanted to ask her what exactly she did other than collect bets and protection money. But it never seemed like the right time and I didn't want her to think I was square, that I didn't get the whole jury-rig, that I was just some Ivory soap kid who took the bus to work and daydreamed about new dresses and dates with men who wore flowers in their lapels.

So I nodded and paid close attention as she talked. I watched how she moved (like she'd thought through every finger lift) and the way she spoke (with care, in the same even tone all the time). I knew I was looking at the big time. I figured she might have to spend a few hours a week in this flea circus of a town, but she was big city all the way and somehow, somehow she saw something *in me*, something in the face like a bar of soap, plain, unshaped, ready for dirt. Made for it.

'So, kid,' she finally said, setting a ten on the table to cover the eighty-cent bill, 'what's your take? You up for a new business venture? One that'll make real use of that stuff I know you have upstairs. You'll learn more in a week than in a decade at the Tee Hee or two decades in the classroom.'

She rose, smoothing her skirt with a flash of the hand and looking me straight in the eye. 'You want it?'

I met her gaze for the first time. 'Yes,' I blurted, standing too, if shakily. 'I'm ready. I'm all yours.'

She nodded and I got the feeling that nod was her version of a smile. 'Good, kid. You did good.'

It was early, maybe seven A.M. I was putting on my stockings, getting ready for my eight o'clock class. Two hours of blackboard staring in a lecture hall filled with yawning bean counters in training. My old man was already out on the route, his egg-daubed breakfast plate waiting for me to scrub.

29

I picked up the ringing phone, tugging a curler out of my hair.

'Do you know who this is?' The voice like a slither.

'Yes,' I said. It'd been three days since our talk and I'd thought of nothing but. 'Yes. I was hoping–'

'Call in sick. You're not working today.'

'Not working? But I–'

But she'd hung up.

Between accounting and business writing, I called the Tee Hee from a pay phone and told Arthur I wouldn't be in that day. I played it real regular, but when I got off the phone, I felt a funny buzzing in my chest. I tried to ignore it, and after classes I went home and cleaned the house, polished Pop's shoes, scrubbed the toilet basin, anything to keep busy, record player blaring to drown out the buzzing, which was loud and, yeah, kind of exciting. Exciting in a way that threw me. I didn't want to think about it. I did two hours of homework and made chops and creamed spinach for the old man.

It was in the morning papers. When the *Clarion* hit the front porch at the crack of dawn, I knew what it would say. It had happened around four o'clock, and only Jerome and Arthur were there, along with a J&B sales rep. Arthur had to go to County for third-degree burns on his face, neck, and left arm. The sales rep was standing near the front window when the bottle came careering in and had to have a couple dozen pieces of glass removed, including one from his eye, which, in the end, they also removed. Lucky Jerome, sleeping one off on the couch in the back office, came out with nothing more than a bad cough.

(But he wasn't so dumb. Later, I heard he left town within forty-eight hours, family in tow. Thirty-five years living in this town and gone in a flash. But hell, he got off easy.)

Later that evening, while Pops was at his regular Benevolent Committee meeting at Saint Lucy's, a police detective came by my house. He had owlish eyes and round shoulders and a wry smile like he'd long ago stopped being surprised by anything. I was ready for him, thought someone might come. I told him I was washing dishes and would he mind if I kept at it while we talked because if they weren't done by the time the old man came home, I'd get a beating. This was a lie – my dad had never raised his hand in all his days, didn't have the brass – but I wanted to keep my hands busy wanted to have something to do while I lied.

'You've worked at Club Tee Hee for how long?'

'Two months.'

'Like it?'

'It's all right. I'm in school. I'm going to be a secretary.'

'So you didn't see a long future there?'

'I was planning to stay a while, sure. It was good with my school schedule.'

'You're a real scholar, huh?'

'What?' I said, scrubbing steak sauce from the prongs of a fork.

'Skip it. You called in sick yesterday,' he said, leaning against the kitchen counter.

'Yeah,' I said, crossing myself with one soapy gloved hand. It was a flashy move, but I took a shot. 'Someone was looking out for me.'

'So what's wrong with you? You look okay to me,' he said, with a vague smile as he wrote on his pad.

I paused, shaking suds off my gloves. 'Feminine troubles,' I said.

He looked up at me. I gave him the stare right back. I had already learned that stare from her. Even then.

He looked down again and wrote something on his pad. 'Can't argue with that, can I?'

She called me later that afternoon. I told her about the cop and what I said.

'Feminine troubles, huh? That what you use to get out of speeding tickets?'

'I don't have a car.'

'Not yet,' she said. 'So I guess you're looking for a new job?'

'I guess.'

'Meet me at fifteen-oh-one North Branston Drive tonight. Apartment 9-G. Nine o'clock.'

It was a tall, pistachio-colored building along the scenic ridge outside of town. The lobby was covered with mirrors and tall, potted plants. There was an automatic elevator with a carpet in it and when the doors opened on the ninth floor, I couldn't hear even one radio, crying baby, or arguing couple. It wasn't like any apartment building I'd ever set foot in.

She was there, ushered me in. The place was big, with a thick band of windows, but there was nothing in it except for a lamp plugged in on the floor.

'Your new digs?' I asked, resisting the urge

to take my shoes off and sink my feet into deep-pile carpeting.

'Yours,' she said. 'You can't live all the way over in Pottsville for your new job.'

'I'm going to be able to lay out rent for this?'

'There is no rent. It's part of the job.'

I looked at her. 'What is the job?' Thoughts of men in hotel suites came into my mind. Men in town for conventions with bottles of rye on the nightstand and loose suspenders. I squinted at her hard in the low light.

'Working for me.'

'Doing what,' I said.

'You don't have to jut your chin out for me, kid,' she said, stepping to my left and looking me up and down. 'Your virtue is your own business.'

She walked behind me, circling me. I felt like a rump roast hanging in Gus's Butcher Shop.

'You're not ready yet,' she said, still looking at me, arms folded across her chest. 'But you will be.'

I didn't say anything. And that was how I started.

The next day, four men from Drucker's Movers showed up with a living room set in maple and glass and a bedroom set in satin blond. As for me, I packed a wicker suitcase and my favorite pillow and bid a dry-eyed adieu to the family manor. The old man wouldn't come out of his bedroom when I left. My sisters came over and gave me a hard time, guessed I was being set up by some married man, called me a whore. I didn't care. I knew I had my ticket.

The first week, I drove. She gave me the keys to a bubble-top Impala and directions first to a locking dock in Deacon City and then, as the week went on, across the state line to a series of warehouses.

'If you get pulled over,' she said, 'you're visiting your sister in Titusville. Her name is Fern Waxman. If they ask to search your car, which they won't if you're worth a plug nickel, then say, Sure, officer, but I'm going to be late and my sister just had a baby.'

No one pulled me over. I watched the speedometer the whole way. I never drove so careful in my life.

I didn't know what I was delivering, not from her at least. Each time I got to my destination, there were always two or three men there. One would ask for the keys and they'd open the trunk. I never opened it, not once.

At the beginning, the stuff was already in there when she gave me the car keys. Once, I snuck a peak when the fellas were unloading. They were lifting a false bottom and pulling out small sacks. After a few trips, I got to see more of the action, cartons of cigarettes, prescription medicine stuffed in long tubes. Once it was tins of Russian caviar, another time, box after box of Star of David pendants.

By week two, I was going to a bank with an ID that said Coral Meeker and emptying a safe-deposit box filled with sparklers like I'd never seen: big, chunky sapphire stickpins, ropes of glossy pearls, an opal ring the size of a golf ball. That time, she had me wrap the pieces in a bag of diapers and baby clothes 'for my sister's newborn.' Other times, I'd use the phony bottom. Once, she had me tuck a stack of passports into the lining of a suitcase. Another time, it was some kind of foreign currency packed tight in a bag attached to a new vacuum I was bringing for this same sister, the luckiest sister in three states.

I did it all just like she wanted. Soon, she saw I was simon-pure and no fool either. I was ready for more. I wanted more.

I was going to the track.

'For this, you gotta look the part,' she said. I looked down at my off-the-rack acid green rayon number, shiny with wear. 'You can't look like a kid eating dinner off a hot plate. You can't look like a table-hopping pickup either. We gotta believe there's nothing funny about big money in your hand.'

'Big money?'

She nodded. 'You ready for soap, kid? 'Cause you're going to be elbow deep in it now.'

I ran a hand over my dress and looked over at her. I smiled for her. I think she wanted me to. I said, Yes, Yes.

Maybe you think during all this I must have felt some pangs of guilt, some doubt. It's true, this wasn't the way I was brought up. It wasn't most families' idea of good girl behavior. Sometimes I even tried to talk myself into feeling bad, into thinking for a second about the regular joes and why should I get away with nice things without working an honest job. But the second always passed and then the seconds stopped coming at all. Truth was, who was getting hurt by my doings, except those who chose to buy cigarettes and booze without sales tax, gamble away their paychecks, skimp their wife by paying back-of-the-truck prices for an anniversary string of pearls? They took their chances and I got the sweet butter skimmed off their bad luck.

It was going to be like my coming-out party. And the getup really mattered. There was a way you had to look at the track. That's what she said. Tasteful picture hats, spare makeup, a few good pieces of jewelry, nothing flashy. Don't want to stand out too much, don't want to be picked out in a big crowd. She took me to her apartment in a sparkling high-rise in the city. She had a walk-in closet big enough for a pair of chairs and a smoking table, big enough for rows and rows of satiny, lustrous fabrics, from gauzy to thick brocade, eggshell to midnight blue. And next to this finery, she had a long row of stiff, tailored suits in pastels. These she wore to the races.

'You save the golds, the patterns, the lipstick red for carpet joints, or for your own time. You want to play uptown at the track, dolly. With the wad you'll have, you gotta look like class.'

So she took me to the big department store downtown, the one with all the mirrors and

38

twinkling chandeliers. Bought me three fine suits – cream, oyster white, periwinkle blue. The skirts hit well below the knee but still fit snug in the right places, because she was no fool. You had to play that angle too, she said. Get a second glance from the high rollers.

She watched me in the three-way mirror of the dressing room. She was smoking a long, gold-tipped cigarette, leaning back in the lounge chair.

'Honey, I got the legs, but your ass is your ticket,' she said, waving her finger to get me to turn around. 'And that rack won't hurt either.'

I looked at myself in the mirror. I could see her behind me, leg swinging. I could see her watching.

On the way home, she told me that my sugar blond dye job had to go. Too late for the hairdresser, she did me herself, peeling off her doeskin gloves. I sat in a chair in front of the kitchen sink, leaned my head back far, and she plunged her jagged-emerald-covered hands through my hair again and again, turning ratted blond into smooth honey brown. I remember looking up at her, into her eyes, husk of creased skin banging over them. Heavy-lidded like a snake. *She's*

39

figuring something now, I thought. *She never stops running the odds.*

We sat in her living room late into the night and she schooled me. Boy, did she school me. She talked to me, low and cool, for hours, never losing her ramrod posture, never raising her voice above her near-whisper. She told me all I had to do was go down to the Casa Mar bullring and place dime bets on a few choice horses. Taking out the racing form, she went through the Friday races and wrote 'place' next to some horses and 'show' next to others.

'You don't want to hurt the odds, so never bet to win,' she said. 'You spread the money around and bet to place and show and you get a return on investment at least seventy percent of the time. That's the stuff. More important, the dough gets cleaned and the tax men only see racetrack winnings.'

She explained it all and made me tell it back to her to see if I understood. Oh did I.

When I was kid, once a year my dad's boss, Mr. Risniak, would invite all his drivers and their families to his big house over in the gold heel part of town. There were frankfurters and hamburger sandwiches and games for kids and the parents all got soused. Mr. Risniak wasn't around too much. He'd usually make an appearance midway through, standing by the barbecue with his sunglasses on, talking discreetly to a few of his favorites, never my old man. I remember thinking he sort of looked like a movie star or a singer in his maroon sports jacket with that poker face. Once, when I was about twelve, I was sitting by myself eating a plate of Jay's potato chips and he came over and sat down across from me. He was drinking out of a tall glass with a lime and ice and he smoked one thin brown cigarette after another.

'Murray's kid, right?'

I nodded.

'So, you get along with your dad?' he said.

I looked up from my paper plate and nodded again.

'Good people,' he said. 'Your dad, he's on the road a lot though, huh? You miss him?'

'Yeah,' I said, looking over at the badminton net. I didn't know how to talk to men yet.

A moment later. 'You're what, thirteen?'

'Next month,' I said, wiping salt from my chin.

'You're gonna be a woman before you know it.'

I could feel my face reddening.

'That's when the trouble starts.' He grinned, white teeth dazzling. 'I married my wife when she was sixteen. She already had lots of boy-

friends. You will too.' He took another sip, then looked back at me. 'You ever have a drink?'

I shook my head.

'Not champagne at a wedding? Well, wine at communion.'

I nodded, trying to meet his eyes.

'Wanna taste?' He nudged his glass towards me on the picnic table, looking around, as if for witnesses.

I stared at the clear glass, tinged with the green of the lime. I pushed my finger against the sweaty side, feeling the cool of it.

'Go on,' he whispered. 'Just one taste, though.'

I kept looking at it, thinking. Then on some kind of hard impulse, I grabbed the glass with both hands and brought it to my lips. It ran down my throat.

Water. It was water with lime.

Mr. Risniak laughed hard, even slapping the table. I set the glass down and pushed it back to him. My face was burning. He took off his sunglasses and looked at me.

'I thought so.' He grinned.

I can't say I wasn't scared, making the hour drive to the big track the next day. Sure, I had the props. I had the drapery, down to silk handkerchiefs in my purse and silk underwear under my new suit, its basting stitches scarcely out. And I had the scratch in nice, clean bills. But I didn't have her attitude, her steel. I felt like a kid knocking around in her mother's high heels.

But I followed orders. I did everything exactly as she said. I checked out the morning line to make sure the odds were where we wanted them. I placed the bets, polite and brisk with the teller. I was careful not to lock eyes with any of the regulars, the daily bettor types who knew the score. 'You don't ever want to be seen with one of them,' she told me. 'Eyes are everywhere at the track. Your cherry is our big advantage. Let's keep it intact as long as we can.'

It was during the second race that I noticed the man watching me. I tried to play it casual. I watched the action. I listened for the call and marked the winner on my racing form. I took out a compact and powdered my nose. But as I peered in my compact, I could see him still watching. A smooth-faced man of about forty-five in a blue linen suit and straw boater, smoking a cigar.

He stayed behind me, eyes on me, for the next four races. By then, it was past time for me to take wing. Teeth gritted, jaw set, I stood up, trying hard not to wobble, to let my eyes dart, to show I even noticed him.

But then he got up too and I felt something twist in my stomach. Was this it? My first real gig and I'm fingered?

'That's a nice hat you have, miss,' he said, standing in the row behind me.

'Thanks,' I said, turning slightly, tucking my purse tight under my arm. 'I'll tell it you said so.'

The man grinned but showed no sign of moving on. Too knowing for a fella looking for a pickup, too smooth a linen suit for a cop. I hoped.

'You play the ponies regular?'

'No, but I love horses,' I said, playing it as easy and as unimpressed as I was with the tipplers who used to hang out by the back office at the Tee Hee. 'You know about girls and horses, don't you?' I added, as if with a wink.

'Only what Catherine the Great tells me,' he smirked, waving his racing form. 'Who'd you put your bills on?'

This sure didn't feel like idle chatter. I didn't like what it felt like. I swallowed hard and hoisted a smile. 'A drib here, a drab there. Mostly, I just like to show off my hat.'

'Can't blame you for that,' he said, tipping his own boater toward me. I was glad my new hand-span sunglasses stopped him from seeing my eyes. Was he a racing commish official? Some kind of private dick? Not a cop, I kept telling myself. Cops don't rate those wing tips.

'If you'll excuse me,' I said, careful to smile. 'I have to be going.'

'Hot date?' He lifted his eyebrows. 'Who's the lucky horse?'

'All my horses are lucky,' I said, turning to walk away, playing it calm, loose, carefree.

'I'll bet they are, honey,' he called out after me as I made my way down the grandstand, slow and easy, like the old lady herself. I knew he was watching me the whole way.

By the time I got to the car, the dapple of sweat on my temples had spread and I spent ten minutes sopping myself with pressed powder and catching my breath. What I wouldn't give for a half a gulp of good whiskey, I thought. I took off my slippery sunglasses and caught a look at my eyes in the rearview.

Goddamn, kiddo, can you go the distance or are you just a tease?

I drove straight to her apartment, like she asked. She was there, a pirate's cache of jewelry spread on her coffee table. Sitting next to her was a balding man in shirtsleeves, a gem scope in his hand. He was holding up an egg-shaped sapphire. Next to him on the table was a small saw blade and some needle pliers.

She tilted her head toward the bedroom and followed me in, not bothering to make introductions.

'Those the rocks I brought back from Rennert Falls last week?' I asked.

She didn't say anything, headed toward the phone. I sat down on the bed, tried to keep a poker face. I hadn't gotten pinched. I'd placed the right bets. Wasn't that enough? How could she know I'd been made anyway? Had I been made?

She dialed and spoke into the receiver.

'So?... Yeah?... Yeah?... That so?... Okay. Thanks, Harry.' She hung up and looked at me.

'I think I did it okay, Gloria,' I said.

She stared at me. I tried to stop my chin from shaking. Why couldn't I be like her, have her ice?

'Everything went like you said,' I added, taking off my hat, poking myself with a pin.

'Did you talk to anyone?'

'As little as possible, like you said.'

'Any fellow approach you? Try to play the wolf?'

'No,' I said slowly. 'One fella tried to make conversation. I don't know who he was. He asked who I was betting on. I didn't give him anything. And I left.'

She folded her arms and kept her eyes locked on me for a few long, long seconds. Then finally, she said, 'You did good, kitty.'

I couldn't fight off the smile. 'It was okay?'

'Yeah,' she said, nodding slow, like a sports coach might do. I felt like the star quarterback.

'So I go back?'

'Tomorrow,' she said, tossing me a meaty stack of rubber-banded bills. 'But next time, scale back the flirt routine. All Harry can gab about is you and your horses.'

I looked at her. It fell into place for me and I saw what a stooge I still was. The man in the boater was a plant, testing me. Christ.

But I'd passed, right? I'd passed. The next test wouldn't be planned by her. It'd be out there, out there in that hot glitter, and I'd have to sink or swim by it.

There were a lot of regular parts of the job, placing bets at the small tracks, moving goods, passing information, making deliveries to and from the casinos. That was my favorite. I loved the swank carpet joints in the big city. I didn't have to go much to the grimy betting parlors in town, or the grind joints filled with suckers, the kinds of places made for low rollers who gave it all up the minute they had it in their pockets. They had regular boys with swollen arms to take care of those rougher places. But the bosses wanted me at the casinos because I stood for something, like Gloria did. I stood for a class operation. Me, the dingy issue of a vending machine man. The girl in the Orlon dress who'd been taking the bus to a chump job just a few months back.

I'd show up at the joints late. I'd head to the manager's office, collect wads of cash all earmarked for the pad. At first, she just had me bring it all to her. I didn't know where it ended up. Eventually, I began helping her make the rounds with it, mostly to the PD, the district attorney's office. There was a

48

complicated formula based on rank and pull and you never let the low-level boys know what the higher-ups were getting, or who else was on the pad.

No one ever gave me a hard time, but every night I'd get invitations, either from the casino fixtures, the bulls, or the hard boys at the door. At first, I was too scared even to one-step with them, to give them back a little of their patter. But the better I got, the more I was willing to toss it around. At least with the prettier, slicker ones. I had a weak spot, right off, for the worst of them. The ones that still had faces worth looking at. The ones without the dented noses or cauliflower ears. Mostly, I had it for the cruising gamblers who didn't rate with the big boys, just threw them their money every night like some nonstop tickertape parade. They were the smooth ones and I didn't mind a little dance with them.

'So I'm guessing you're the soft spot at the end of the day for some very sugared daddy.'

'I'm not so soft.'

'I could rub you some round edges, you give me half a sec.'

'I bet you could. From the way you've been chasing losses all night, I can see you're a born grind.'

'I can take being called a grind player long as I got some odds on seeing you grind a hurdy-gurdy for me one of these eves.'

Yeah, okay, it wasn't Lunt and Fontanne. If these fellas could really give you a line, they wouldn't be at a casino every night, losing their shirts.

Besides I never let it get far. At the toniest joints, I'd once in a while let a butter-and-egg man buy me a steak. For his troubles, he'd get a dry kiss on the cheek. And when it paid, I went on dates with the high-stakes gees. But I never laid for one. I really felt like I could keep coasting like this, above everything. She taught me how you could move through it all and not let your feet sink in it. Not let your fine snakeskin stick in their muck.

You have to decide who you are, little girl, she told me once. *Once you know that, everyone else will too.*

We were sitting in her plush pink and gray living room. I remember looking at her under the milky cast of the brass wall sconces, looking at her while she passed on pearls of wisdom (*You always want to know the strategy behind it, honey. You do things for them without knowing why, there's nothing in it for you.*) and I'd think maybe I was getting to see what she was like back in 1945, bright-eyed, rosy-cheeked, slinging those gorgeous stems one across the other and making hay while times were good.

I'd look at her and I'd think about all the stories. The favorite tale among the boys at Club Tee Hee was about a New Year's Eve party at a big penthouse in the city back during the war. She was the hot ticket back then and she shimmied with every hood in the place, making rounds, drawing all eyes on her. Finally, one of them asked her to put her money where her mouth was. Story was, she threw her head back and laughed, saying, 'I'll put my mouth where the money is,' and made her way to every man in the room, on her knees. On her knees.

Word spread through the party and, after everything, one of the mobsters' wives came up to Gloria, called her a whore. With the strongest arm this side of Rocky Marciano, Gloria slapped the wife around, grabbed her by the hair, and tugged her against her chest, growling, 'I'm the best damn cock-sucker in this burg, and I got the rocks to prove it. Your knees have rubbed plenty of carpets. Where are your diamonds? Where are they?'

Or so the story went.

Now that we were close, I thought maybe I could ask her about it, so I did. I must have been crazy, drunk on the low lighting, the hour upon hour of cigarettes and shoes off, legs tucked under us as we sat on opposite ends of the sleek mohair sofa. She looked at me like I was a goddamned fool.

'That was Virginia Hill,' she said, stubbing out her cigarette. 'Hillbilly tramp. I got better things to do with my mouth.'

I wasn't really sure what that meant, but it shut me up.

I shouldn't have believed it anyway. It was hard to imagine that much hot blood running through her. If she had a man in her life, I never heard tell. The job was the life. Four decades of carrying money, getting high rollers to place sucker bets, moving swag across state lines, and adjusting odds for the boys working the policy racket all through the east side. She herself was proud to say she'd never in her life laid down a bet on her own nickel. *I'm no chump. I know the odds. I make them.*

So, I followed her example. I wore the clothes, I did the jobs, I followed orders. All business. And no matter how many shiny-haired swains pressed against me, I never played around. *Be the lady,* she told me. *They beat their wives, they beat their whores. I never took more than three socks from one of these goons in all my years. That's why. Be the lady.*

'But didn't you ever fall for one?' I asked once, sucking on a swizzle stick and hoping for some sign of soft in the old lady, something beating under the finely pressed shantung suit. 'Sure, kid,' she said, eyelashes grazing her cheeks. 'There were a few. I lived this life, you know. But I watched myself and I never mixed business with anything else. There were men, but not these men. No. Straight men. Straight enough. Men who may not have lived by the book but lived by some book. In this life,' she said, crossing these glorious gams, shimmering in the filmy light, 'you can't let your guard down. If you can control yourself, you can control everyone else.'

But then there he was, as if on cue.

It started with the furrier.

Her name was Regina, a little five-footer with a perky chest, a beauty mark, and a funny twitter in her voice, like a comic-strip French streetwalker. The fur shop in the lobby of the Ascot Hotel sold her wares. And the Ascot Hotel was on my rounds. On its top floor, in a series of connecting suites, high-stakes poker and baccarat games drew big crowds of serious players seven nights a week. There was a bar, girls, the whole bit. I used to make pickups there and I'd see Regina now and then. She'd make her way upstairs sometimes, on someone's arm or to appraise a fur piece someone was staking.

One night she caught me in the powder room. Twitching her nose as the party girls sprayed themselves with Chanel No. 5, she slunk next to me and made a gutsy pitch.

'I love the mink-lined gloves you were wearing last week,' she cooed. 'I could make you a hat to go with them. No charge, of course.'

'Why so generous?' I said, hardly looking at her in the mirror as I reapplied my makeup. 'I don't know you from Eve.'

She smiled, lipstick thick and bright. 'I've seen you around a lot. I know who you are. I got something I want to bend your ear on.'

'My ears don't bend,' I said, heading toward the door. Yeah, by now I was head of the class in Gloria Denton's Charm School. It was like walking around with armor, bulletproof. Nothing could touch me.

'Listen,' she whispered, rushing up behind me, following me out to the bar. 'It'd be worth your while.'

'How would you know how much my while is worth?'

'Believe me, I know,' she said eagerly, eyelashes swatting. 'Ask around about me. People'll vouch for me. I'll wait.'

So I mentioned it to Gloria the next evening, careful to sound neither excited nor too casual.

'Yeah, I know her,' she said, turning the steering wheel. We were headed to Googie's Chop House, where we went most Friday nights. She liked to order the London broil, although she never ate much of it or anything else. Anything that didn't line her pocketbook really wasn't worth her time.

'So could she have something?'

'Light me one, will you?' she said, gesturing toward her cigarettes. I put one in my mouth, lit it, then tucked it in her mouth. She took a deep puff. 'She runs with a pretty high-tone pack. Makes pieces for society coin. She might have a hot steer. Open your ear, see what she pours in.'

I didn't have to go looking. When I got to the Ascot the next night, Tino, the concierge, said there was a package waiting for me. I opened the rose-scented box and there under the pink tissue was a hat of Black Cross mink, lined with satin the precise crimson of my evening gloves.

Sure enough, she was upstairs, chewing on a curly-foil toothpick at the bar, practically chomping at the bit.

'Thanks for the lid,' I said, setting the box down on the bar next to her.

And she walked me through it, made her case. The setup looked airtight.

It was like this: There was a family in Highcrest Hills, a few miles out of the city. The Duttons. Their fortune came from Dutton bread and muffin mixes, that cheap stuff you find on grocery store shelves all over the state. The boxes with the freckle-faced kid with his tongue hanging out of his mouth.

They were big money and Regina delivered her custom-designed skins to the lady of the manor every season, red beaver coats and blue fox hats in the winter, brocade coats with Chinese leopard trim for spring, ermine wraps for cool summer evenings, ponyskin suit jackets and short chinchilla coats for fall. It was endless.

But fur was the least of their riches. The big loot was in jewels. Mama Dutton was a jewelry hound and Papa Dutton was built to please her.

'When she'd look at my furs,' Regina told me, 'she'd pull them out and drape them over each piece to see how it looked. Three-, four-, five-carat rocks. Big pendants and stick-pins the size of snowglobes. Heavy-banded chokers and thick charm bracelets, chunky brooches, enough rings for a hundred fingers and toes. All prime-cut.

'So last week I delivered her latest skins in time for her spring passage to Old Europe. Rome, then Capri, don't you know. She wanted them fast because they were leaving Saturday. Last Saturday. Gone for four weeks with only a skeleton crew of servants holding down the fort, keeping their half-drunk eyes on Bluebeard's stash. And nobody knows the gold mine that's up there. Who figures? They sell biscuit flour.'

I was new to this kind of game, but it looked awfully good to me. I passed the info on to Gloria and Gloria corralled the talent and within four days the Dutton domicile had been hit. They tied up the housekeeper and the groundsman, while the safecracker went to work on the two wall safes Regina had eyeballed. It only took him ten minutes and, in twenty, they were out of the house. Sure, they had to get a little rough with the groundsman, had to crack him once and he lost some teeth, or so the papers said, but otherwise, it was as clean as they come.

And my finder's fee was a tidy treat. I bought myself a charmeuse dress but the rest I spent on her. I wanted to give her something. And I wanted to pay for it myself.

I went to her favorite high-end antique store, the one with the green baize walls and full afternoon tea for customers. I wasn't so flush I could match her tastes, but I knew I could find something and when I saw the letter opener, it said class all over to me. It was old, the guy behind the counter promised me that, and with his half-specs and his tweed suit, he looked like he knew what he was talking about it. He took it out of the case and set it on a velvet tray for me to eyeball. It was shaped like a sword with a sword's sharp tip. But the handle had a fancy design in bronze, two heads crowning the handle tip, each with curly, snaky hair, facing each other.

'Who're they supposed to be?' I asked, touching the coiling curls.

'It's the same woman, looking at her reflection,' the man said. 'Art nouveau. It's an excellent choice.'

'It might be two different women,' I said, squinting.

'If you like,' he said, smiling as I took out my billfold.

She was keen on the gift. Anybody else might not be able to tell, but I could. She looked at it a long time and a few days later I saw it in her bag in a pale gold sleeve she must have had made special for it. She used it every time she made her bank pickups, slicing through the paper and counting the bills out with fluttering gloved fingers. I knew I'd done it right.

You see, I wanted to show her that I knew if it wasn't for her, I'd still be stuck with my head over the ledger at the Tee Hee, postponing the inevitable roll in the sack with Jerome or Arthur for a shot at a bigger paycheck. She saved me from all that. She turned me out and you never forget the one who turned you out.

But it wasn't made for forever. I didn't have her stuff.

The thing was, the whole deal with the furrier turned out to be bad business. It gave me a taste for more when all I could think about already was getting more, getting my hands on, and in, more. It'd been so easy and the paycheck so big. Why, I'd be a chump not to look for other chances, I figured. As much as she'd given me in the ten, twelve months I'd worked for her, I was already looking to up the ante. If I'd thought about it, I'd've been ashamed of myself. But I didn't. I just kept going.

Never fuck up, she told me once. *That's the only rule.*

'You've never made a mistake, not one, in all these years?' I asked. 'Mixing up numbers, late to the track, one drink too many and you start talking too much to the wrong fellas?'

She looked at me in that icy way of hers.

Then, in a flash of the hand, she tugged open her crepe de chine jacket, buttons popping. There, on her pale, filmy skin, skeined over with thready wrinkles, I saw the burn marks, long, jagged, slipping behind her bra clasp, slithering down her sternum.

'How–,' I started, my mouth a dry socket.

'A state trooper pulled me over for speeding downstate,' she said, palm flat on her chest, patting it lightly. 'Made me open the trunk, tapped the sham bottom, and found sixty K in hot rocks, each one a fingerprint.'

'But that wasn't your fault,' I said.

'I should have been more careful,' she said. 'I learned the hard way. The boss then, the big one, he watched while one of his boys did it. Pressed me against a radiator until the smell made us all sick.

'I learned the hard way,' she repeated. 'Now you've learned it easier. You don't need this on your fine chest,' she said, fastening the mother-of-pearl buttons. 'So don't fuck up, baby.'

'I won't,' I said. 'I won't.' And I meant it.

But he was the one. I could feel the way it was going the minute I saw him losing his shirt at the tables. Loose and easy grin and a gambler's slouch, a back-patting, hand-shaking way of moving through a room. But when his eyes narrowed on me, his smile disappeared and I could feel him. I could feel him on me. My palms itching, I rubbed them together. I could feel it everywhere, something sharp pulsing under my skin. *I'll crawl on hands and knees for this one*, I thought. *I can feel I'm going to be on my hands and knees for this one.* He saw it on me too. He figured fast he had the upper hand. He was the first man I ever met.

Things got pretty crazy right off. I couldn't help myself. I let him do whatever he wanted. Who was I to say no. There was nothing he could do that I didn't want. Not even that.

Okay, I'll tell you how it went. I was making my rounds at a new casino running in the lower level of Yin's Peking Palace. It was my last stop of the night and I was tired. She was on a plane east that night for the kind of big deal I wasn't let in on yet. Now that she had me around, she had a lot more time to do fancier jobs for them. Once, one of the jewelry fences told me they had her flying to Switzerland, but that seemed like movie stuff. I didn't buy. The operation was big but it was still small potatoes compared to the networks running out of Chicago, New York, Miami. I knew my bosses had bosses and even they had bosses.

Point was, I had no place to go and it was only one o'clock. I figured myself for a whiskey sour and a walk around the joint to see what was flying. Maybe I'd stumble upon something. I'd been hoping the furrier might pop up. It'd been three weeks since the deal went down and maybe she had something new cooking.

What was great about walking around these places was that, by now, people started to know who I was. At the track, I had to be discreet, blend in. But at the casinos, I was there to show myself. And people took notice. The men and women both. Sometimes, you'd hear the regulars trying to explain who I was to one of the newer marks.

'She's Gloria Denton's girl. She works for Gloria.'

And if they didn't know who she was, they weren't worth anybody's time, might as well be in the back alley with the dishwashers, giving up their coins at three-card molly.

That night, there was a lot of action at the roulette wheel in the back. Somebody had a real spinner going. Larry, the manager, was standing by the table, which meant whoever was winning was winning big enough to demand a close eye.

I slipped through the crowd of spectators, all eager to catch some of the luck. That was when I saw him standing at the table, eyes on the felt. All black mick hair and sorrowful eyes and a sharkskin suit cut razor sharp. He had some candy on his arm, a sometimes-pay broad I knew from the lobby of the Fabian Hotel.

Spin after spin, he must have pulled in close to a grand, big money in these parts. It was like he'd set off some kind of crazy energy in the air around him. I liked it, but not that much. Not yet.

'Golden numbers,' Larry said to me, quietly. 'Would you look?'

'Gaffed wheel?' I said, eyeing the croupier, who was sweating the attention from his boss.

Larry shook his head. 'That's Vic Riordan. He's no worry of mine. He taps out here every night. He practically pays my salary. And yours. Or he would if he ever had more than a red cent when he came in the door.'

'Looks like his luck's changed.'

'Don't count on it.'

And Larry was right. Just when everybody

was urging him to stop, to walk away while the table was still hot, the guy gave the crowd a smarmy smile. 'What, I'm gonna rathole after this streak? If I'm gonna lose, it's gonna be here with Mama,' he said, winking at the dealer.

Sure enough, he did start to lose. And then he kept losing. The gaudy-colored stacks got smaller and smaller, the crowd slowly drifting away, and before I knew it, it was just Vic Riordan, his whore, and me.

I couldn't stop watching. Something about the way he just kept going, never seemed frustrated, never lost his temper, just kept sinking, sinking.

It wasn't until he'd watched his last four chips disappear behind the croupier's rake that he seemed to notice me. He looked over with a funny kind of smile. Not like a man who'd just won and lost Blackbeard's booty.

He looked at the wilting lily on his arm. Her head darting around, she was eyeing greener pockets. 'Some lucky piece,' he said to her. 'I need something shinier. All your shine's rubbed off.' She shrugged. He shot a smirk my way. 'There's the metal I need in my pocket.'

I took a sip from my glass and didn't say anything.

'Don't you owe me a drink for the show?' he said. 'They should name a church after me after that sacrifice.'

'You'll rise again,' I said, turning to leave. Already though, I didn't want to go. His patter was nothing special but there was that kind of crazy bravado, a drowning man wondering what the water would do to his new suit. Still, I started walking.

He didn't follow. I thought he would. So I left the back tables, but I stuck around the joint. Which meant something. I watched some baccarat, sucked on some pretzels, asked around a little about the furrier, caught some gossip about a new carpet joint opening in the back of an appliance store downtown.

He was at the bar when I saw him again.

'Someone bought you that drink,' I said.

'You can always find a few knee-bending Catholics in these places,' he said, raising his glass lightly. 'They'll always do a favor for a wayward soul.' He put a hand on the leather stool beside him and cocked his head.

I didn't move. I felt like something was turning.

'Come on,' he said. 'Let's get drunk. I want to see you with a hair out of place.'

His grin did me in.

Before him, I'd never fallen for one. Never bothered to look up for one that wasn't just a money clip to me. In all my girl years, I'd only rolled pro forma with high school boys, office boys, head knocking on Adam's apples in backseats, mouth dry and raw. By their closing shudder, I was already snapping my garters back up and biding my time for the finer things. All the ones before Vic Riordan, I was just killing time. They never made me want more.

I wasn't drunk and neither was he. But we were standing by his car in the parking lot of Yin's. We were leaning close to each other. It was coming on three A.M.

'It's too bad you're such a kid. Otherwise, I'd take you home. Mess up that fancy girl posture. Bend you back a little, you know?'

'Who says I'm a baby,' I said. 'I've been in long pants for years.'

'Are you kidding?' He put his hand on me, just above my chest. 'I bet I could smell Mama's milk on your breath.'

'Come close. I'll open wide and you can see. No milk teeth.'

He moved closer and his smile reminded me of the wolf in bedtime stories. When I was a kid, whenever my sisters would tell me fairy tales, running their fingers up my arms and legs, I always felt it for the wolves. Narrow eyes, teeth glittering like a handsaw. The wolves were waiting, but you had to put yourself in a dangerous place first. You had to play your part. I would dream myself into the thicket, swinging a basket, whistling a tune, waiting for the growl, the flash of yellow eyes, the sudden pillage, the blood tear. The wolf got you where it counted.

When Vic got close, that's what it was like. I'd invited him in, with his sharp cologne, his darting eyes, his pockets empty of chips, all his spoils gone by night's end as if he had holes in the lining, which, in a way, he did. He was a loser, straight up. A chalk jumper. A sucker bettor. But his hands. His hands tore me to ribbons and left me that way.

I should be ashamed. I should be filled with shame. That night, right off, he had me.

There I was in his apartment, half past four. Nothing in it was paid for, not the chrome and leather sofa, the mirrored coffee table, the thick buff-colored drapes, not even me. I gave it to him without so much as a steak dinner, a wilting rose, a smooth line. Let's face it, he broke me because I was begging to be broke, his hand so hard on my shoulder, my shoulder so hard on the sofa, I couldn't steer the Impala for a week without gasping for air.

The next day, I had to pick her up at the airport. I was feeling all nerves. I'd been late for some of my appointments and had forgotten to make two drops the night before. Scrambling all over town to catch up, I could hear her voice in my head, *See what happens? See how quickly it falls apart if you don't keep your legs together?*

Walking across the tarmac, she looked tired and pleased. When she got in the car, she tossed me a box wrapped in bright tissue. I opened it and it was a pair of long silk gloves in pearl gray. She had a pair like it from some famous glovemaker back east and I was always talking them up, always complimenting her on them.

'Gee, thanks,' I said, feeling, I'll admit it, a pinch over my chest. I felt like I'd done something lousy.

'Let's go get some dinner, kid. Some lobster and pink champagne,' she said, smoothing her hair back. 'Things are really cooking with gas. I got an eye for talent, that's what they're saying Upstairs. The more they see the way you roll, the more honey for us both.'

All through dinner, I kept saying to myself that I hadn't done anything wrong, not yet. I wasn't going to let it get in the way, not like she might think. Besides, I might never see the fella again.

But I knew I would.

And I knew, somehow I knew, that it couldn't help but interfere, that I couldn't help but lose control of it. I wanted to lose control of it.

That night, as we toasted, I got dizzy with the endless champagne, the rolling piano at the supper club, the fine food prepared tableside, her glowing face. It was glowing like I'd never seen before. With her, you couldn't tell with laughter or smiles or words even. She didn't wear it like that. You could tell from something in her that came out once you knew her bone deep like I did. I knew her bone deep and I could see that she was so happy she was glowing. And I wanted to cry. I sat there and I wanted to cry. But I didn't. She'd already schooled me long past the point of crying. I was better than that. Instead I smiled for her, laughed for her, and was beautiful for her. It was the best dinner I ever had.

I never let her see me with him those first weeks it was going on, hotter and crazier every night. I finished every run before I hightailed it to his place. Some nights, she had to do numbers late for the new dog- and cockfights over in the warehouse district. They were nasty bits of business and we never had to show up at them, no woman would (*Not even women like us,* she said and I didn't like the way she said it). On these nights, I was supposed to go to her place after my last rounds. Impatient to get to Vic's, feeling things in my hips just thinking about seeing him later, I hurried as fast as I could to help her look for hits, envelopes from all over the city spread across her glass coffee table. She always wore her gloves when she did it, not to hide her worn hands, not from me, but because she knew where the betting slips had been, grimy candy stores, shylock newsstands, back kitchens, bowling alleys, those same down-at-the-heels warehouses where the fights were held.

Her gloves, in one of a dozen shades of white, rose, pale yellow, danced along the envelopes, flipping over the slips, looking for the matches. She was fast, and I was getting fast too. And I never said a word to her about him. I knew what she would say. *You lost it, you little bitch. You lost it. You can't discipline yourself, you're of no use to me.*

But what could I do? Three, four in the morning, I'd find myself driving over to Vic's place to see what would happen. To see what I'd do. He was always waiting for me with a smile, his collar open, a drink in his hand, a quick line about how he almost had it, almost scored a big pot. How if I'd run into him a few hours before, I would've seen him with bills falling out of every pocket. I told him I didn't care. I told him I didn't care at all. I dared him to show me what I would do. He liked dares.

One night, he ripped my $350 faille day suit from collar to skirt hem in one long tear. Fuck me, I was in love.

I'm yours, that's what I told him without ever spitting out a word. He could see it on me, feel it on me. He liked to have me on the bare mattress, liked the way it rubbed me raw. I liked it. Liked the burn of it. Liked thinking of it all the next day, every time I leaned against anything, every time the strap on my brassiere pulled across it.

It was like – it's not a thing I like to say, but it's the way it was, I tell you – like at mass. After kneeling so long on the warped wood floor. Some of the rabble used the flat pillows Saint Lucy's set out. Not me.

If you don't feel it cracking your knees, your spine, was it really praying? Was it worth God's time to listen?

If you didn't feel it on your body long after he'd left, was it really worth laying for him? I wanted to feel it.

I didn't know what he saw in me, I didn't care. I was crazy about him and it made me feel tough, not soft, like she might've thought. I felt a hardness in my chest as I made the circuit, chin-wagging with the runners, the casino managers, the controllers. Nothing could touch me. That's how I felt. Except when I was with her. When I was with her, it all fell to pieces and I had to set my jaw, steel my spine, build myself up new again.

But you couldn't just keep on losing like Vic did, could you? If anyone knew that, it was me. I saw it happen every day. I was never involved in the part of the life that was about consequences. She wasn't either, not anymore at least. I heard, sure, I heard a lot, about the old-fashioned kneecap-busting, the gut punches, the head batterings, worse. And I saw it with the way the Tee Hee went up in flames (only to reopen, three weeks later, as the Swizzle Lounge, doing bang-up business even as I steered clear, super-stitious).

Still, I told myself I was keeping it all con-tained. It was organized and I had it under control. I only saw him at his place and everything that went down went down there. And I did all I could to make sure she never saw him. I knew if she saw him, she would know I'd gone for him. I felt like it was all over me, all over my face. What I didn't realize was that you're always on borrowed time when it comes to these things. She could have told me that, if I'd've listened.

It turned like this;

It was a Friday afternoon and I ran into Vic at the Casa Mar track. I didn't know he bothered with the showplace baby bullrings they sent me to, the kinds of places that blew a ton on their overhead for hoity-toity banners and grandstands trimmed like layer cake, all to draw society green. But there he was, and the minute I saw him, I got nervous. If I'd had half a second, I might have walked in the other direction. He was just the kind of dyed-in-the-wool day player I shouldn't be seen with. I had to look clean. But he'd already spotted me.

'I didn't know you came out in daylight, little girl,' he said. As he got close, I could smell him, the bay rum and smoke and everything else. I felt things stirring in me and I had to hold on to the rail to stay standing. As much as I felt it each night when he opened the door to his apartment, I felt it ten times more here, off guard, under the sun, with people pressing against us, shouting, the energy wired through the whole place.

'A girl's gotta get herself some sun,' I finally managed, trying to steady my voice. 'And a chance to wear her brand-new hat.'

He looked up at my broad-brimmed society sun-catcher. 'And it's a damn fine one, honey. They coulda used you on the *Titanic*.'

He was standing closer. All I could think of was what she would think seeing me here with him, with a guy like him. In front of everybody. Everybody with deep pockets who laid money out for sin in three counties.

'How 'bout we go behind the paddock for a minute, have a smoke?' I said.

He looked at me and I saw a glint of teeth flashing. 'Sure, baby, sure?'

That wasn't why I wanted him back there, by the jockey quarters. But once I was there he had me against the back wall and no one was around and I won't tell you about what we did. I don't want to tell you about it, but it was in the daylight and I was on the job, and when it was over, it took me ten minutes and two cigarettes to stop my knees from shaking.

God help me, I was weak. Strong as I felt, I was weak.

That was when he started talking about the hole he was in. With a shark named Amos Mackey, a big-time fella, a comer with stakes all over town. I knew Mackey, though I didn't say so. You couldn't miss him. A barrel-chested swell fond of three-piece suits and bright pocket squares, he owned five red-sauce Italian joints and a couple of watering holes and he had eight, ten guys working for him just to keep things moving smooth. *He's going to give our page-turners a run for their money one of these days*, she once told me. *This town can't hold him.*

And he meant business. Mackey had big grins for everybody and could glad-hand it with every gray-suited businessman this side of the chamber of commerce. But I'd heard enough back-alley talk to know that if Vic had dug himself a hole with the man, he'd better start filling it with bills or, as they say, he'd be filling it with something else.

'I know I'm going to hit soon,' he said. 'So I'm not that worried. But I hope it's right around the corner. I can't dodge his boys forever. They're slow but not that slow.'

'How'd it get so bad,' I asked, stamping out my cigarette on the hitching post.

'Ah, I had such a hot tip. Inside-inside, you know? From this gal who holds hands with one of the trainers. She said it was all wrapped up. The jockey was on the take and only a few people knew. The bomber was going down and this hot new Bismarck was going to take it all.'

'And that sounded like a sure thing to you,' I said. God, these guys are my bread and butter, I thought. How did it come that Vic could be one of these guys? Why couldn't he be as smart as his hands?

'As sure as it gets,' he said. 'Believe me.'

I wondered how much he knew about what I did to think I wouldn't know better.

'But the bomber didn't go down,' he added with a shrug. 'The jockey, he didn't take the dive. Changed his mind, I guess.'

I didn't say anything. What could I say? Didn't he get it? There were no insider tips. Not for guys like him. You couldn't win and if you did, it wouldn't be for long. That's why they call it a racket.

So he told me how the major-league loss put the scare in him. He'd needed big money fast. So he hustled and borrowed and played again. Sometimes, at blackjack, the dog track, he won. But it didn't matter. Instead of paying off the vig, he tried for more, he played it up higher, just like I'd seen that night at Yin's. And it was a big slide from there. He just kept dumping it all, on overhead tips, bad tips, tips everyone knew were fixes. Hell, I dropped those kinds of tips. It was my job. They were all junk.

'Why don't you just lay off the scene for a while,' I said. 'I'll help you make some touches. We can scare up enough to get him to lay off and...' I was going to suggest he, get a job for a while, some paychecks, but it seemed crazy even to mention. It hit me Vic probably hadn't worked a day in his life. What kind of job could he get? What kind of job would he take?

'Thanks, baby, but I don't work that way,' he said, lighting a cigarette for himself. 'If I can't make it happen fast, I just blow town. Got some connections out west. There's a lady I know. She's flush and has it bad for me. Wants to marry me. She'll help me out. She's my escape hatch.'

He was looking at me and I was looking at him and I wouldn't give it to him, wouldn't give him the satisfaction. But sure, I felt it. I was made of blood and guts. I didn't want him hightailing it to some other woman with some big house on the ocean while I stayed here and slept alone.

'But I doubt it'll come to that,' he said. 'I got a feeling.' He tapped his chest, ring catching the sun. Teeth flashing. 'Something special's coming my way.'

'I know that song,' I said before I could stop myself.

He laughed. 'I bet you do. But baby, I mean it. I'm not one of those sad sacks you see at Yin's, the poor suckers on a beeline from casino to poorhouse. I got bigger stuff in me. Sometimes I can feel it rushing through me, just standing there watching the wheel, the hand. Don't worry. You'll see.'

There was something in his eyes, something flickering. It got me going again, my

79

throat throbbing. It was something about not being able to stop himself, about going all-in, with each game, each race, each hand, each spin of the wheel, with everything.

I just knew I had to get out of there fast before things got crazy again.

'Okay,' I said, my voice barely there. 'I'll see you tonight.'

I wanted to go home after seeing him, to pull myself together. But the rules were the rules and I had to go to her place. I had to give my report and she had to pass me some messages for my rounds that night. The whole way there I kept thinking about what a bad move I'd just made, not just being seen with him but doing what we did. And then to hear about the mess he was in, which made him a bigger target. A fellow that deep in the hole, she might hear about it.

I thought about stopping for a drink to get my head back on straight. I didn't want her to know I might be losing it. I didn't want her to know I'd gone so crazy, and all for a sharpie, a plunger racking up big losses every day, even when everyone who mattered knew how it worked, how he'd never make it that way, loading it all on one horse, one race, playing the wheel all night, falling for sucker bets.

But if I had a drink, she'd know. If I stopped at all on my way back, she'd know. She knew everything.

When I got to her place, she was pretty busy, which made it easier. She was on the phone bawling out some guy who'd boosted some jewelry and then gone ahead and tried to pull the rocks from their settings himself.

'Okay, Mr. Gemologist, what do you think we can do with these geegaws now?' she said, waving me in with her hand. 'Our guy says each one's got a chip in it. What makes you think you know what the hell you're doing? What'd you use, bolt cutters?'

I sat down on the sofa, back straight, and waited. Watching her, hearing her lay down the law in that way of hers, voice so cold you prayed for her to yell instead, I got to thinking about how I had to do better, had to get my act together.

She hung up the phone and walked toward me. 'How'd it go?'

'No problems. Smooth sailing.'

'You're a little later than usual,' she said, sitting down beside me. And as she did, I felt my chest go tight. I thought maybe –

81

what a thing to think – that she could smell him on me. Could she? Could she do that?

'You know, brushing off a fella or two,' I said. 'Is that for tonight?' I pointed to a manila packet on the coffee table.

She looked at me. 'Yeah,' she said, slowly. I thought for a second, was she leaning in toward me? *His bay rum, his cheap cigarettes, everything else.*

But then she sat back, reached over, and picked up the packet, tossing it over to me.

'Yeah, that's it. I want you to make three stops. First, over on the west side...'

I could hear her voice in my head, low and cool. *You want to throw it all away? All for some hard arms, some hot hands on you.* But who said I took a vow of chastity? Who said I couldn't control it? It won't interfere, I told myself. The minute it does, he's gone. If the boys can have their high kicks, garter flashes on the side, why can't I have something too? Something to get my heart going, chest heaving. *Can you hear my breath go fast, even now? Christ...*

The next night when I got to his place, I could tell he was half in the bag, stinking of Jim Beam. He wasn't a big boozer, so I wondered what was doing. 'Baby doll,' he said, collar askew, grin wide, 'I've been redecorating.'

As I followed him into the living room, my heels slipped hard into long ridges in the carpet.

'Trail of tears, baby,' he said genially. 'All that's left.'

That's when I noticed the living room furniture was gone.

'Repossessed, as they say. Like I was one of the spooks who plays your policy games.'

'The store or Amos Mackey?'

He laughed, shrugging. 'You got me, beautiful. It was all gone when I got back from the Rouge Room. So I figured I'd celebrate my ... liberation from material possessions.'

He was talking too big, even for him. I read it like this: he's a lot more shook up than he's been letting on.

He took my hand, jamming my fingers together painfully. 'I figured *we'd* celebrate.'

'The Rouge Room, eh? Moving with real high rollers now, are we?'

His eyes narrowed, just slightly. 'What, you think I can crawl outta the cuff I'm in by laying down fins at the Coronet Dry Goods cockfights?' There was a new, gravelly tone in his voice.

I brushed by it, hadn't seen him hot under the collar yet and didn't want to. It looked like it might not be pretty. 'So how'd you do,' I asked, setting my bag down on the windowsill.

'I did okay, Ma,' he said, trying for teasy but not meeting my eyes. He turned toward the bottle set on the radiator and poured me a paper cup full. 'You know what kept distracting me, though?'

'What?' I asked, downing the drink.

'This little redheaded number next to me was blowing dice for her man and I could see down her dress.'

'I get it.'

'No you don't. Nothing special, believe me. But she was wearing this baby blue negligee under her dress. I could see the lace on the top edge.' He poured me another and took a swig himself.

'Yeah?'

'Well, baby, damned if it wasn't just the

color of this vein…'

'Vein?'

'You can hardly see it, but it's there.'

'On me?'

'Yeah you.'

'So where is this vein?'

He moved closer, bottle still in one hand, pressing my stomach. With the other hand, he pushed me against the windowsill, then reached down and tugged up my skirt. His hand was there and then gone.

'Right here, baby. I can feel it now. I don't need to see it, 'cause I can feel it right here. Can you?'

'Yeah.'

It was Friday late afternoon, an hour before I met up with the old lady for our weekly dinner. My head was all jammed up about Vic. I kept thinking maybe there was something I could do without showing my cards. Maybe buy him some time. But I didn't know Amos Mackey like that. And if I did, I couldn't risk it getting back to Gloria.

The only dealing with him I'd ever had was a month or two back at the While-a-Way Cocktail Lounge. I passed by his table on my way to talk to the owner in his back office. As usual, he was surrounded by grinning municipal types and buying rounds, shaking hands like he was running for mayor, which maybe he was. When I got to the office, the owner, a real deadbeat, started griping about his payments, complaining about the boys who collected it. Everything. He was giving me a song and dance.

Finally, he wrung his hands at me and moaned, 'Sweetheart, don't you see? If I have to pay that kind of protection, I'll have to close.'

I looked at him and shrugged. 'If this'll kill Grandma, then Grandma must die.'

He paused for a second, then waved his hand at me. 'What, I'm supposed to be scared by a little broad five feet two, eyes of blue?'

'Smarten up,' I said, hand out. 'You know it's not me talking to you now. I think you know who's talking.'

When I walked out of the office, envelope in hand, Amos Mackey was right there, you couldn't miss the teal green suit and the inch of canary yellow fluttering from his breast pocket. He'd been making a phone call in the stand-up booth. He glanced over at me and hung up the phone.

'You're Gloria's, right?'

I didn't say anything, just finished tucking

the envelope in my purse.

'I like it,' he said, nodding, the ghost of his smile there. 'I like it.'

That was it. My only dealing with Mr. Amos Mackey to date. It was something, but not enough to get a sit-down with the man over a bridge jumper with a vig you could choke on.

Then I thought if I could put Vic wise to a fast-money operation, maybe there'd be a shot. Maybe the furrier...

So I headed over to the Ascot to see if I could get a line on her, see if she was going to be around that night. Walking through the lobby, I went by the Ladies' Boutique first. That was when I noticed a red squirrel stole in the window with a placard that read Furs by Fiona. I ducked inside and asked the tall blonde at the counter about it.

'What's with Furs by Fiona? I thought Regina had the works.'

The blonde shook her head. 'Regina won't be peddling her buckskins anytime soon.'

'What gives?'

'Didn't you hear?' She looked at me, eyebrows raised into perfect half-moons.

'Hear what?'

Lips glistening, she leaned forward eagerly. 'Depends on who you talk to, but she's pulled an Amelia Earhart.'

'Yeah?' I was surprised. So she got her cut and skipped out while the getting was good.

'Some say she got into some trouble and took a powder. Others say, if so, why is her apartment still full of clothes and things.'

'Who says that? How do they know what's in her apartment?'

The blonde shrugged, leaning back. 'Some people were looking, I guess.'

'Looking for what, honey?' I said, squinting at her. What kind of game was she running?

'How should I know,' she said, retreating. 'I hear things.'

I nodded. Seemed Regina was involved in more setups than she could handle. A real player, that one. You had to admire it. If she'd gotten out still standing.

I went upstairs to the casino. It was too early for any real customers, but I thought maybe if I poked around, careful-like, I might get the word on Amos Mackey and how rough he played. As long as I didn't mention Vic's name, there was no tying him to me.

The closest I got was a whisper from Stitch, one of the stickmen. He was setting up for the night with that kind of orderliness

88

you always see in those guys, the good ones.

'Yeah, Mackey's a player. You don't need me to tell you that.'

'So not someone you want to be racking up vig on?'

He looked down at his chips, smoothing them with his smoke-yellowed hand. 'No, my dear, you do not.'

'Meaning?'

He looked up at me, eyes hard and clear. 'Go ask the folks buried under three feet of concrete in the wine cellar of Arnos's Italian Grotto.'

'I'm guessing they aren't talking.'

He grinned mirthlessly. 'No, but I guess you could ask Manny, who runs stick over at the Tattle Lounge.'

'The guy with the eyepatch?'

'He got lucky. His wife cashed in some bonds for him before the other eye went pop.'

The warning bells were ringing from all corners. But as loud as they were, I couldn't do anything about them. Even if I could figure an angle on how to help Vic, it would mean shining a light on me with the old lady. Running to put out one fire would start another. Sure, there was one fix. Stop seeing the sharpie. But who was I kidding? He had a hold of me. He had a hold of me and as much as I wanted to stop, I didn't want to stop. I couldn't go back. He had something on me. He knew my number and there was no turning back.

She picked me up at nine to head over to Googie's Chop House. I was so distracted about Vic and what I'd heard, I wasn't careful. Sliding across the bench seat of her El Dorado, my skirt rode up and she got an eyeful. Five bruises, glaring through my stocking, dotting my thigh, an oval for each finger, in a perfect radial pattern.

Green, violet, raw, hot to the touch. Yeah, I'd seen it in the bath that morning. And when I got dressed. My palms itched every time I looked at them. I could feel them throbbing.

At first, she was silent. Then she switched gears and began pulling away. 'Who did it,' she said. 'Who did it to you?'

'I got caught in a turnstile at Casa Mar,' I said, pulling my skirt down.

She looked at me for a second, flinty severe. I found myself counting the faint lines crimping her crimson mouth. A line for every lie told to her by a two-faced shill like me. Then she turned her eyes back to the road, gloves wrapped lightly on the steering wheel.

I knew she didn't believe me. She could read everybody, most of all me, who she'd made from scratch. She'd given me my poker face, molded it herself, so she knew it when she saw it.

It wasn't until two hours later that she brought it up. We were in one of the round booths in the back and she'd had three vodkas, two more than I'd ever seen her drink since I'd met her. She didn't seem tight. Instead, the booze seemed to make her sharper than usual, more focused, her words barreling across the table at me. We were talking about other things, business things, when suddenly she set her glass down and looked straight into my eyes in that way she had, her neck curved toward me, jaw forward, like a cobra hood. It always got my pulse going.

'Listen, baby doll, somebody hurts you,' she said, 'they don't get a second chance.' Then she slid closer, so close I could smell the ambergris in her perfume, the expensive vodka on her tongue. 'You're mine,' she said, putting one gloved finger on my thigh until I winced. 'Roughing you up is roughing me up. And I don't let anyone rough me up. You're mine and someone puts his dirty paws on you they might as well be on me. You're my girl. I won't think twice.'

And I knew she meant it.

It was scarcely two days later when it happened. Guess I knew it was coming, could feel it in my gut even if I didn't let myself think it out loud. I'd been talking myself out of worrying. She'd backed off. Hadn't asked me who the guy was. Part of me was worried maybe she didn't need to ask, already knew, had known all these weeks. But she wasn't pressing me, so I could make myself believe. I hadn't explained the bruises. I let her think whatever she thought.

But as for him. As for the powder keg he was sitting on, he was betting, dodging, and losing his way straight to the basement of the Grotto. And when I came by his place Sunday night, late, there was no answer at his door. For the first time in thirty nights or more. So then I thought about Amos Mackey's boys and got spooked. I took a bobby pin from my hair and popped the lock, a trick one of the loading dock fellas had taught me once in exchange for a gratis box of Old Golds.

The furniture was still gone except for the box spring he sugar-tongued the landlady into advancing him, but his clothes and toiletries were there. And there were no broken windows or signs of trouble. But I didn't feel much better. I couldn't exactly call around the casinos asking for him. So I decided to stay put.

In the end, I fell asleep waiting, nearly set myself on fire with the cigarette I'd left burning between my fingers. There was light coming through the windows when he busted in close to seven A.M.

'Sorry, baby. Sorry. They took me for a ride,' he was saying as I tried to open my eyes, straighten my back. I peered across the room and at first all I saw was the spray of red on the side of his face, as if he'd opened a cherry soda pop too fast.

'Mackey's boys,' I said, rising.

'Who else,' he said, voice raspy, broken, not his usual smooth, fast jabber. I walked toward him, eyes coming into focus. It looked like he'd been sideswiped, half his face and neck crusted with drying blood, the side of his head pocked with a nettle of oozing cuts. I stood in front of him. It seemed like I should help, but I wasn't sure how.

'They smashed me with a bottle. I guess it knocked me out. I think I was out for a long time. What time is it?'

'I don't know,' I said, my head wavering tentatively over the side of his face. I could see small bits of green glass glittering amid the stubble. 'You need stitches, Vic.'

'Fuck stitches,' he growled, backing away from my hand, shoulders drawing up. 'Don't you get this? You of all people should get it. This is it. I'm out of turns. This was the last warning before limbs start coming off. These boys are choppers and you know it. You know it.'

I felt the color sinking from my face, but I stood my ground. We never talked about my job, about what I did. I couldn't help what he'd heard, but I never told him anything straight out. 'Listen, Vic, I don't know Amos Mackey. Only to see him. I–'

He rolled his eyes. 'Can the schoolgirl routine, angel. There's no more time for dancing.'

'What do you mean?'

He grabbed me by the arms and looked me in the eyes, his battered face glaring

94

sticky red. 'I gotta get the big man thirty Gs by Wednesday or finito. Get it now?'

I didn't say anything. Would they really go from a bottle smash to a dustoff? They wanted their money, after all. My mind still reeling from the size of his cuff – thirty thou, Christ, Christ – I tried to think. But I paused too long and he was in no mood to wait.

'I said, *do you get it now?*' And as he said it, he shoved me backwards, hard.

Without thinking I shoved him back, hard.

His eyes showed surprise and that was when he covered his face with his hands and I thought for a second he might start crying like a baby. But Vic was no milksop. He'd been this close to God's acre before, I could tell. There were no tears, but the light did go out of him for the first time since I'd met him. No more gleam in his eyes. He tugged at me, put his arms around me, went on and on about how he was sorry, how he knew I was the only one he could count on, all that.

I took him to the bathroom and we tried to clean up his wounds with the rusty old first-aid kit in the medicine cabinet. He let me put a stitch in and I pretended it was like basting a skirt hem. It wasn't. Then I made coffee. We sat on the box spring like a couple of hoboes and drank it.

Slowly, he came back. The Vic from before. Jaunty, ready for anything, and sure, I knew it, a washout, a chump. He was going to chase losses until someone caught up with him, roll his dice into his own grave sooner or later. But as much as I knew it, I couldn't help myself. He was finally laying it on the line for me. He started up his patter again, but this time it was right to the chase. If I didn't help him, there was no helping him.

And he came clean that he knew what I did, he knew my job. He was mostly interested in the bets at the track.

'Listen, sweetface, didn't you ever get tempted?' he asked, eyes flickering eagerly.

'What do you mean?'

'You know,' he said, playful.

There it was.

'Come on,' he wheedled. 'You got more smarts than any girl I ever met. You're telling me you don't think about the long green to be had if you're willing to veer from the script?'

Busted face and all, he was smiling. All-in, that was Vic. Before I could say much, before I could react to the pitch, the pitch that I knew was on the tip of his tongue, he looked at me, head to toe. He took my coffee cup from my hand and tossed it on the floor. He was touching me again. He lifted my skirt, wanted to see the bruise, which had turned three colors since Friday. 'The thing I'm going to do,' he said. 'It's going to mark you worse than that. But you won't see it. You won't see it. You'll just feel it.'

His hands on me, what could I do. I wanted more. I was the chump. It was me.

After, he finally got to the sell. Turned out this tout had passed him a tip on some sports scheme that would mean a big payoff for Saturday's game. College football, what the hell did he know about it? You don't have to know about football, he said. You just have to know the fix is in. Some thick-headed fullback was taking beans to fumble deep in the other team's territory and tip the point spread.

'A lot of fellas have gone to the state pen for that,' I said. 'And the rest got suckered by players who decided not to do the dance when they got on the field.'

'I'm telling you, this is for real, Bo Peep,' he said, splaying his hand eagerly on my chest. 'These guys know their stuff. They're master point shavers. They had fourteen basketball players on the pad all last season and made out like Rockefellers.'

'Point shaving is a long haul. You make it slow, game by game. You don't get a big score just working the spread on one game.'

'You do if the game is right. This is a big one, two corn-fed rivals, a ton of action, and Hayseed U favored by thirteen points over Podunk State. Believe me, this one adds up right. Sure, I'm not walking away in the chips, but I save my neck.'

'But what good does the tip do you,' I asked. 'You got, what, two hundred clams left to stake? I can give you what I've got holed up in my mattress, but that still wouldn't get you to the promised land. Not even close.'

'That's the beauty part,' he said, smile spreading across his face like a thick rubber band. 'Don't you see? You're carrying a fat handbag to the track that day. Can the dime bets and let it all ride on Hayseed U.'

I felt my mouth go dry. This was it. He was really asking me to do this. He was really doing it. I shook my head back and forth and started to laugh. And then I couldn't stop laughing. He didn't like it. Didn't know what to make of it. I covered my mouth with my hand, tried to stop.

'What's so funny, bright eyes?' he said, grabbing my face. 'What's so goddamned funny?'

'Nothing's funny,' I said, pulse pounding, body shaking. I felt like I was all nerves, they were shooting through me, bursting just beneath my skin. 'Nothing's funny at all. Don't you see? It's crazy. My head would be on a pike by day's end.'

It would. Didn't he know? He couldn't know because he didn't know her. What she had up her sleeve, inside her silky gloves. How she could see what I was going to do before I did it. Because she scripted me. She did, not him. Couldn't he see that?

'So it's not you that does it,' he said, shifting gears quickly. 'Supposing, baby doll, you get mugged on your way to the track? It's no one's fault. Could happen to any slip of a girl who makes her way among sharpers and trouble boys.'

I paused, looking down at my hands, at the big cocktail ring, the size of a pearl onion, a gift from her after I soft-soaped a state trooper out of popping my trunk.

'It wouldn't help you, Vic,' I said, spinning the ring around my finger. 'It's pin money. Even with all the bets I make, they're so small, they don't add up. It doesn't work like that.' I wanted to crawl the walls. These types always figured I'd be laying down a million each day because the money boys could really rig all the races, dope up all the horses but their pick, crazy stuff like that, and so if they just knew which way to bet...

Vic, he was a dreamer, see. You had to see that in him and when you did, it had a charm that worked on you. You wished things were like he wanted them to be. They weren't.

'So when do you carry the most coin? Leaving the high-tone casinos? When the box man walks you out? I know you don't do the major pickups, but you take the vig, don't you?'

I looked at him, rubbing my sore arms, my raw arms. Because I knew. Hell, normally it really wasn't that much cash, and when it was, I had protection. But I knew damn well that she was going to be gone overnight on Friday and I'd be making double the betting rounds I normally did, the small track and the big one. It was more scratch than I usually carried and sure, it seemed like something they'd have a hard boy do, but she'd been burned before by crooked delivery boys. I was the only one she trusted to do it. It wasn't thirty big ones – no one was going to let a 105-pound frail carry a roll like that – but it was enough to make a dent.

He could see me thinking, weighing. He was trying to get a read on me, see which lever to pull to make the lights flash, make the cherries line up three in a row.

'I mean, sugar, you gotta think about your future. Don't you see? There's sweets for you too. Down the line.'

'What do you mean?'

He smiled and cocked his head. 'This arrangement's a long game, like you said. They got two bean stalks on college basketball teams, another quarterback. I can set it up. You can bet solid the better part of the year and get yourself some fox furs, some chinchilla. I'd like to lay you out on a full-length sable, one with all the teeth still in it.'

'What makes you think I want a piece of this?'

He shrugged and smiled. But he didn't say anything.

I reached down for my shoes and slid them on.

'I'm going for some cigarettes,' I said.

His eyebrows lifted. 'Okay. But ain't that the fella's line?'

I could tell he was worried I wouldn't come back. But he also seemed wired up, edgy, hopeful. He thought he had a line on me. Maybe he did.

It was still early and as I walked, I was the only person in the world. All you could hear was the click of my metal-tipped heels on the pavement. It was just me and this. This thing. And I knew it had all been headed towards this from the minute she set her hooks in me, from the second I took the bit in my mouth, eager, hungry, ready.

By the time I reached the newsstand four blocks away, the owner dragging open the rusty shutters, I knew I was going to do it. And it wasn't the promise of bullion. It wasn't even, or not just, Vic. Vic and the things he could do to me and the things I wanted to save him from. There was something else at the bottom of it. Something dark and swampy I couldn't look at, couldn't face. But it had to do with her. It had to do with her. What would it mean to try to take her on, beat her? What would it be like to smoke-and-mirror the queenpin herself?

(And she had never opened herself to me. She had shown me what to do, how to do it, but she had never let the veil drop, the mask fall. If she had done that ... if she had done that...)

(And this too, wouldn't it mean we'd be closer even than now, thick as blood, because it would bind us forever in some way? It would either be the secret thing, the only thing I would keep from her, or if she found out, it would be the thing that would bind us forever, like locking horns in battle, bound in blood.)

I bought a pack of Chesterfields from the newsstand vendor. My hands shaking, he matched me and I smoked one on the spot. As he clipped the string off stacks of dailies, he glanced at me.

'Rough night, honey?'

'Had to make a big decision,' I replied.

'Who's the lucky fella?' He smiled, hands covered in newsprint.

'Luck's for suckers,' I said, letting the cigarette fall to the ground.

Back at his place, his hand on my hip bone, my hip fast on the mattress – fuck me, who knew I was so easy? Who knew I'd pull a Judas the first chance I got?

If I'd waited it out, if I'd been patient, bided my time, looking for just the right chance, then I could have done it right. I could have used all the lessons she taught me to plan it perfectly like she would have. But that wasn't what this was. It wasn't about out-smarting her or about protecting myself. I had to do it fast because there was no time. I had to do it fast before I lost my nerve.

'You can't throw any money down on horses, Vic,' I said. 'If they find out I got heisted, missed making my bets, *and* some-one scored on the same races, then it's all over for me, Vic. Do you see? They can con-nect the dots and it's over. Tire iron to the head.'

'Sure, I see, baby, sure,' he said, practically rubbing his hands. The wolf. The wolf but not like before. His eyes not yellow flares trained on me. No, in his head, he was standing at that roulette table, letting his chips roll across his fingers, watching the wheel whirring, everything in his body vibrating with its purr, with the clicking of the spinning ball, the other bettors holding their breath, leaning in, pressing on the polished wood at the table's edge, the wood groaning as they squeezed it with their anxious fingers, nothing moving but the wheel, the ball, and a comet trail of cigarette smoke twisting up to the low, low ceiling.

'There's this rhythm,' he once told me. 'Each dealer has his own, like a signature, no two alike. Every time they pick up the ball from the pocket, they do it the same way. Every time they spin it, it's the same way, with the same go behind it. If you know the dealer, if you know him well enough, watch him close enough, well, the ball will always spin the same number of times and will land the same number of pockets away from the last spin. It becomes a song you know and you can sing along with it. You see, there's ways to make it all work for you, babycakes. There are. You play like I do long enough, it's going to pay off, the big gold dream.'

He was every pit boss's, every racetrack owner's, every shark's deepest dream come to life. He was going to talk himself into losing for the rest of his days. He was a fish, a pigeon. Might as well walk into the carpet joint with his pockets hanging out of his pants.

Funny how it almost made me cry, it was so beautiful. Who could keep on believing like that? I'd never believed anything like that.

'You have to promise me, Vic,' I said, and my hands were shaking. I knew I would be seeing her in an hour, taking her to the train station, and how could she not see it all over me? 'You have to promise you'll only bet on the football game. Nothing else. I hear you place bets at those tracks–'

'Don't worry, honey,' he said. 'I'm playing by your rules. Cross my heart.'

He was so calm, so pleased, so distracted, thinking not of me but of that big gold dream of his. Suddenly I wanted to smack him. I almost did. Instead, I blurted out, 'She'll never buy it. Don't you see? My boss, she won't believe it. I wouldn't.'

He smiled and took my arms in his hands, focused his eyes on me. 'She will. She will. You just gotta make it look real for her. You gotta look like you were taken.'

I looked at him and then I said it. I knew it fast and said it. 'You're going to have to put me in the hospital.'

Before I picked her up, I had a vodka neat, then, in the same glass, a slug of Micrin

106

mouthwash, neat. By the time I was driving her to the train station, my hands were still, my voice was steady. I matched her mask for mask. In my head, I'd talked myself into forgetting everything but doing my job. Pleasing her. Seeing her off.

Just as we pulled into the station, she said, 'What's going on?'

I felt something spring in my chest like a kick drum.

'What do you mean?'

'You seem relaxed,' she said, powdering her nose from a small tortoiseshell compact. 'Figured you for more jumpy.'

'Why should I be jumpy?' I said, trying not to suddenly sound jumpy.

'Because, Little Miss Marker,' she said, snapping the compact shut, 'when I'm heel-and-toeing it for a few days, you usually are.' She looked at me. 'Don't tell me, you're all grown up now, kid?'

There was a kind of warmth in her voice, not like anyone could notice it but me, but I could, I could hear it and it seeped into my ear like honey. I couldn't see her eyes, not with those big sunglasses enclosing her face, narrowing her face into a kind of arrow's head, her sharp chin the point. It was just a mask anyway. That face was just a mask.

Listen to the voice, the voice is the thing. Not the usual slither, or jagged edges or grit clenched teeth. There was a warmth. I heard it, felt it.

'Maybe I am grown up,' I said, trying not to smile too much, to make too much of it, to cause her to retreat. 'Or getting closer.'

'Off your knees at least,' she said, opening the car door and stepping out. 'You're off your knees at least, aren't you?' she said as she slammed the door behind her and began walking away.

I sat in the car for five minutes trying to figure that one out. Then I stopped trying.

He didn't pause a second before his fist came at me, a hard belt to the jaw that snapped my head against the wall with a nasty pop. I saw stars. I remember thinking, *I figured this would be harder for him.* It wasn't hard at all. Then, before I knew it, his left came at me, swiveling my head the other way, cheekbone cracking against the metal door frame of the clubhouse. I thought I would be sick. I held my stomach with both hands. Everything was tingling and I was still standing and I felt everything everywhere.

'Give me one more. Give me one more,' I

whispered, chin raised, face hot, whole body shuddering. He paused, gave his brow a crinkle of worry, but for less than a second, then let me have it. That was the one that knocked me out.

It had all happened so quickly. An hour before, I'd picked up the money from the accountant over on the east side. I didn't see anyone watching me as I left, but I wasn't taking chances. It had to look real enough. The usual routine was to go straight to the track, so that's what I did.

We'd talked about how Casa Mar would be crowded, jammed with spectators. Most places, we'd have to do too much playacting and there was the risk of someone playing hero, seeing it and saving the day. Then we hit it. More than once, I'd walked behind the paddocks, having a cigarette, listening for any useful back-fence chin-wagging. So we made it so I'd stroll just far enough from the mix, behind the jockeys' quarters.

Standing there, I lit a cigarette, and two puffs in, it was clear the time was now. He came at me. He came at me hard. No one was watching. We'd both made sure. But from far enough away it would look real. It would look like an ugly holdup.

When he came at me, there was this: he was the wolf again. The yellow flare in his eyes. His hands on me. And he was all-in. I remember thinking, *He's hitting me like he'd hit a man,* and I wanted to take it that way, oh, did I. I also remember thinking how it was like being back at Saint Lucy's, where your whole body is prone, your whole body is ready to take it. Because that's why you're there.

He wasn't supposed to knock me out, Vic. It would make it harder for me to avoid the cops, a ruckus. I didn't want a ruckus. Even if I had been mugged, she wouldn't like that, wouldn't like all the questions.

A wandering horse trainer found me as I was coming to, helped me to my car. He wanted to take me to the track docs, the track badges, but I told him if my husband found out where I was, he'd do me worse than the mugger ever did. So he let me go.

The whole drive, scared I would pass out again and crash, I gritted my teeth so deep into my lip it bled. But it kept me awake. I went straight to her doctor, just like I would have done if I'd really been clipped. He said I should have gone to the emergency room. He talked about contusions, a crushed cheekbone, and how he hated to see girls in this line of work. He put three stitches above my eyebrow – Vic hadn't bothered to take his ring off either – and gave me a shoebox full of dope.

When I got home, I didn't look in the mirror. I knew it would pass with her, it had to. Who would do this to herself on purpose?

The only nagging fear was that she might think whatever fellow had put the bruises on my thigh had now knocked the face out of my face and taken my money. Which was true, after all.

When she called that night, I told her. I told her I'd been jumped at the track by some gee who must've been following me, waiting for his shot.

'You went to see Haskins?'

'Yeah, he wrapped me up.'

'Gave you some Mr. Blue?'

'Yeah.'

'Cut the booze then,' she said. I could hear her exhaling. 'I told you about tails,' she went on. 'About where you walk and when.' Then, after a pause, she said, 'Funny.'

'What?'

'That today of all days it happens. It's like they knew you were carrying twice the action.'

'Some people might've known.'

'My accountant's clean,' she said, rough. 'I've known him thirty years.'

'I didn't mean it like that,' I said. 'My head's fuzzy.' I let my voice go soft, weak. It wasn't hard. I was feeling the gluey rush of the morphine I had taken an hour before, in preparation.

'Get some shut-eye,' she said. 'I'll get a cab from the train station and be over first thing in the morning.'

When she saw me, her eyes widened. It was the first time I'd ever seen the whites of her eyes. Her jaw was trembling so slightly like a violin string. So slight only I would notice. Because I'd never seen it any way but granite still.

I was lying on the sofa, curled up in my bathrobe. I was Camille.

'I'm sorry,' I said. 'I'm sorry.'

She walked over. For a second, it looked like she was going to place one gloved hand on mine. It hovered there. She was letting me see something, but just barely.

'He came out of nowhere,' I murmured. 'I should have made him. It was like he came out of nowhere.'

She sat down on the coffee table facing me.

Taking off her sunglasses, she peered at my face. I felt like something behind glass, something smeared on a slide under a microscope.

'I'm sorry,' I repeated. 'You have to know. It won't ever happen again.'

'No,' she said. 'It won't.'

I didn't like the look in her eye. 'Please, Gloria. I'll make it up.'

'I know,' she said. 'I should have taught you this. I should have taught you how to handle yourself for this.'

Through the throb over my eye I looked at her. She was nervous. For her, this was nervous. A little twitch on the side of her mouth, her arms straight at her sides, fingers closed around the edge of the table. For her, this was as bare as it got. It seemed like a good sign. Like she was figuring things, how to work it so we didn't take the hit for this.

'You can still teach me that,' I said, trying to sit up, my face pulsing like a separate, living thing. 'Teach me how to handle myself.'

She nodded at me. 'All right,' she said, 'but for now, stay put.' And she reached down for the afghan hanging off the edge of the sofa. She lifted it with her gloved fingers, pulled it up my chest.

I could hear her breathing, hear her thinking. *How am I going to play this with the big boys?* That's what she was thinking. *How'm I going to save my girl?*

'I'll take care of it,' she said as she left.

No word from Vic, but that was probably smart. We knew we had to be careful. Had to bide our time. The next day I went to the drugstore for the football results. The man who sold me the paper tried not to look at my face when he gave me change.

'Who was favored?' I asked, pointing to the score.

'State. They were favored by thirteen. Won by six.'

'Okay,' I said. I would have smiled, but it hurt too much.

She came over later in the day with some more dope and some groceries.

She didn't look so nervous anymore. And she didn't like my face. She kept staring at it and shaking her head.

'You can't make any runs until your face heals. You look like a two-dollar whore.'

She wasn't going to be tucking me under any afghans today, that was clear. I wondered what she'd found out.

'I know I can't,' I said. 'In a few days...'

114

'Go back to Haskins tomorrow. Have him try to do something. Christ.'

We had some coffee. She told me she would have jobs for me in a week or two. Until then, I'd have to lay low. I asked her about any fallout from the bets I hadn't been able to place. I was sure her bosses weren't happy paying off a higher return rate to bookies whose bets they'd covered as place and show.

'Nobody's happy,' she said. 'But I told you: I'm taking care of things.'

As she was leaving, she turned to me, slipping on her leather driving gloves.

'You know,' she said, 'the action at the track that day – somebody won big on the fourth race. The way some might see it, the tough who robbed you ended up playing that dough. All on one horse. I have a lot of eyes at the track and they're looking into it for us.'

'Good,' I said, because there was nothing else I could say.

I think I probably already knew Vic had played at least some of that money at the track, even with his sweet football tip. He couldn't help himself. He had to take every shot he had. He couldn't turn away from a sure thing. All his life was about sure things.

Oh, Vic.

He finally called the next day.

'I saw your game played out real nice,' I said.

'Yeah, baby.' I could hear his smile. 'And there's plenty more gold to mine there.'

'So you put the whole haul on the game?'

'Sure did. Just like we said, buttercup.'

'And so now you're true blue with Mackey?'

'True blue, baby. So can I see you? I been thinking about you. About the catch in your throat you get... About your–'

'I'm not exactly pretty as a picture,' I said. 'Besides, it's too risky.'

'Okay, baby. You'll let me know when it's time. I'll be waiting.'

'Yeah, Vic. I will.'

When I hung up, I knew three things. First, he'd either bet some or all of the dough at the track, or he'd gotten some kind of payoff from passing on what he knew about the odds at the track that day Second, he hadn't settled up with Amos Mackey. At most, he'd paid an ounce of vig to hold off the baseball bat. Third, he was now in the hole deeper than ever. If I were putting money on it, I'd have bet he'd lost every last thin dime at one of the grind joints the night after he'd collected big.

All for nothing, I thought, pouring myself a vodka chaser to go with the morphine haze. If I skate out of this, if I make it, that's it. Here on out, I only bend for her. I only got ears for Mama.

You get one, I kept saying to myself. *That was your one.*

The next evening she was taking me out to dinner. She said I'd been through a lot and I deserved it.

The night before, I'd dreamt of things happening to me, to her. Every story I'd heard about her, every story she'd told me about them, the bosses, came back in shards, piercing sounds. Faceless men in black cars running me down, long blades and hinges of skin, shotguns in my face, and the smell of my own flesh against the radiator.

I knew I had to shake the fear. It was all over me. I had to shake it. I had to play it regular.

She'd made special reservations, she said,

at the swank new Venetian Gardens. 'It's one of Amos Mackey's new joints,' she'd said on the phone. 'He's on the move, that one.'

'Is that so,' I'd said as flat as she ever taught me.

I wanted her to see I was on the mend, would be ready to dance for her again soon. I troweled a thick layer of Pan-Cake over my mottled face. Looking in the mirror, I watched as the creamy Amber Rose erased all the Technicolor, leaving everything smooth, molded, like the pinch-face Nancy Ann Storybook doll I had when I was a kid.

Before, even with all the bruises, the sunken cheekbone, I had seen myself in the glass. I could look in the mirror and see me. Now, with the makeup leaving only slits for eyes, it was like that face was gone and in its place was something else. Someone else. I knew who else.

She came over at nine P.M., dressed head to toe in sharky silver.

'You look good.' She nodded at me. 'But this is an occasion. And occasions call for little extras.' She lifted the garment bag in her hand. 'You can wear it tonight.'

I smiled, feeling the Pan-Cake crack slightly. 'But I don't deserve this. I don't deserve anything.'

She looked at me and shook her head. 'Don't sweat it, kid. It's just one twist in a long seam. Don't worry your black-and-blue head over it.'

She must have seen the relief in my eyes, my slitted eyes, because she added, 'You don't give me enough credit, baby. I don't leave you hung out to dry. It's not good business. And besides, you're my girl.'

Her garnet lips curled, slanted into something, something like a smile. The closest to a smile she came. I smiled back. I felt like I must have been crazy to do what I'd done to her. After everything. She was the one in my corner. The only one.

'Now let's go celebrate,' she said. 'Toast your recovery. Let's paint the town.'

She lifted the garment bag high, like a fisherman showing off his biggest catch. 'We're going to dress you to kill,' she said. 'You gotta show 'em you're not down for the count.'

I said okay. I said I'd love to. I was hers.

In one long stroke, she unzipped the garment bag and the shimmering red dress gushed out.

'With your fox,' she said. 'It's meant to go with the platina fox.' The one she'd bought me for my first night of casino rounds. My favorite piece, silvertips hand-dyed by Regina, when Regina was still around.

I slid out of my sheath dress and felt her hand touch my still-raw back as I stepped into the gown. The neckline hung low, weighted down with heavy beading like scales against my chest. We walked over to the long mirror in the corner of the room. She stood behind me, six inches taller, that crown of titian hair and those eyes thin as dark threads punched in her face.

We stood there a long time. I could feel something was happening. It was razoring in the back of my head without coming to the fore. The way she was looking at me.

She laced her silver gloves across my collarbones, eyes trained on our reflection in the mirror. It was as if she was saying to herself, *This was me once. I guess I'm a thousand years old to you, I've seen it all. But look. We're the same, we're the same. I made you. Sometimes it's as if I made you up inside my head.*

I watched the red panels splash against the silver of her suit. My teeth were clattering. I looked in her eyes, the lashy slots. Were those my eyes? Would they be? Those eyes, they knew everything. Everything.

I felt like we would be locked like this

forever, pressed against each other, front to back, she with one sharp stiletto jutting between my stocking feet. The red dress tight across my breasts, my hips, her hands splayed across my throat. That's when I got it. This was it. It wasn't me and her. We weren't the same. It was me and Candy Annie at the ladies' room in the Breakwater Hotel. The one who got it with a straight-edge razor, gutted like a flopping fish.

But I couldn't move.

Maybe I didn't want to.

'I hope he was worth it,' she said, even as her mouth was still. 'Was he worth it.'

Her arm came forward and I saw that bronze letter opener in her gloved hands. She held it to one side of my throat.

I'd like to say I said a Hail Mary or something like it. But I didn't. The pointy tip grazing a throbbing vein in my throat, I just shut my eyes and waited for it. Waited for the warm jet, the feeling of my body sinking. I was ready. But it didn't come.

'You're lucky I'm soft,' her voice rang out, loud and rickety. Not her voice at all. I opened my eyes as she dropped her raised arm to her side. With a shove, she knocked me down and my knees hit the floor with a familiar crack.

'Gloria, I–'

'Hell, I put in good time with you. I gave you a year. I'm not throwing it away just because you can't keep your legs together when it comes to two-bit pikers like your boy Vic Riordan.'

I let myself slide completely to the floor, curling a hand around my neck. She was still holding the letter opener and it was at my eye level. It kept catching the light.

'How did you find out?' I managed.

She let her head fall to one side mockingly. 'Oh, kid, you know better than that. How couldn't I have found out? Imagine my disappointment with how easy you got caught.'

'You tailed me?'

'Amos Mackey got me wise weeks ago,' she said, grabbing her handbag and dropping the letter opener in it. I was glad to see it go. 'I'd already figured you were giving it up to some sharpie. It was written all over your face. Your body was twisting with it. But I didn't know who it was until Mackey told me.'

'How did he know?' I asked, sliding back against the front of the sofa.

'He had a tail on your lover boy. He wanted his money. He saw you going into

Riordan's apartment every night, coming out an hour later with your stockings in your hands. I never pegged you for such a round heels, Tinker Bell. I thought I'd snagged a good girl from a long line of fish eaters.'

I didn't say anything.

She looked down at me. Looking at me seemed to rock her all over again.

'Get off your honeyed ass, little girl,' she spat. 'Put on your coat.'

'Where are we–'

'You know where.'

We were in her car. She made me drive. It was a fifteen-minute ride to Vic's, which didn't seem nearly long enough to talk her out of anything.

'What are you going to do, Gloria?' I asked, keeping my voice steady. She was moving in this queer, jerking way, not her usual measured gestures, her slow turns, the methodical way she'd open and close her purse, light a cigarette, get into a car. As I drove, she kept coiling around in her seat, her mouth hooked across her face, a strand of hair, no two, slipping from her chignon, catching in her mouth.

I didn't recognize her. She wasn't the Gloria I knew, but maybe she was the Gloria

I'd heard about. The one from those stories they told at the Tee Hee. I felt a phantom pulse in my neck where the letter opener had pressed, its two-headed handle nestled in my jaw.

'Mackey's boys will take care of him, Gloria. He's in so deep, he–'

'Like hell I'll leave it to them,' she tore out at me, voice deep and guttural. 'He tangled with me. He's going to answer to me.'

'But why put the heat on you,' I said, counting on her endless practicality, her all-business style. 'Why draw the spotlight–'

'This is the gink who beat you raw like street trade,' she snarled. 'He's going to see what it's like to be ridden.'

Hearing that gave me a window in. Seemed like maybe she didn't know how Judas I was. Didn't know I was a game part-ner in the setup. Well, let her go on thinking that way. Looking at her blood-rimmed eyes, who was I to correct her? If she was almost willing to slice me just for being a doormat girlfriend, who knew what she'd do if– Well, that meant bad things for Vic.

'But I never want to see him again,' I tried. We were a half mile away and time was run-ning out. As much as it was looking like Vic had played me, I didn't want to unleash her on him. Besides, who knew what he might say to her about me? Back against the wall, he could start spilling like a stuck pig.

'I don't give a damn what you want,' she snapped. 'You had to lift your skirt for him. For that bridge jumper. Every gal in town has his number, but you, you can't help yourself?'

I didn't say anything.

'Even at your age I knew who was worth letting into my bed,' she said, voice shaking. 'They had to show me the velvet. They had to show me they were standup. They had to show me their stuff. I was careful, do you see? I was discriminating. That's how you last.' Then, more quietly, 'That's how I lasted.'

It was the closest she'd ever come to showing me something. It wasn't heat, but it was something. Maybe her forehead burned above room temperature once. Maybe she'd once felt it like you couldn't stop it, like a thudding, aching thing.

We were at Vic's building. I tried one more time. 'He knows Mackey's boys are after him. He's probably skipped town.'

She looked at me like I was a prize sap. Which I was.

'He might have a gun,' I said.

She kept looking at me, but something

125

was shifting in her face. Something burning behind her eyes. something roaring up. It was like she couldn't stop herself now, like she could taste hot blood on her lips. Here was her heat, I realized. This was her heat.

She was breathing so hard the pearls around her neck were wobbling with each exhale. Patting her handbag, she said, 'I hope to hell he does.'

My hand shook as I knocked. She stood several feet away. Don't open it, Vic, I kept thinking. Don't be there. He knows Mackey's goons are ready to take their pound of the flesh, he can't possibly be sitting in his apartment like a slaughterhouse lamb.

'Look who busted out to see me,' he said, grinning at me as he opened the door.

'Vic,' I started, but before I could get a word out, she was behind me, shoving me in the apartment in front of her. Vic's eyes went wide as she slammed the door behind her. He even backed up a few steps.

'Isn't this a surprise,' he said, voice still steady. 'Gloria Denton. Your reputation precedes you. I feel honored—'

'Cut the theatrics, flannel mouth,' she barked. I stood slightly behind her and she seemed, suddenly, to be ten feet tall in the small space. *This room, this room where you let him ... where you did that...*

I couldn't look him in the eye.

'Your skin game's over and look what it got you,' she continued, waving her purse around the empty room.

'I don't know what you're talking about,' he said, smiling foolishly 'But I'm awful glad to see my girl. You chaperoning now?'

'Vic, don't–' I started, but her eyes flashed at me and I shut up.

'You cheap clip artist. You think you got any business laying your flyweight hands on my girl?'

His eyes narrowed a little, his pose became stiffer. 'She wasn't complaining.' Then he turned to me. 'Were you, sweet-face?'

His eyes fixed on me, he took a step toward me, and I could smell the bay rum, the Old Golds. I'd like to say I didn't feel it in my knees. But I did. Of course I did.

I did terrible things with him, Gloria. I couldn't help myself. I want to say I regret it but I don't, not even now. Not one dirty thing. I loved them all.

She shot a hard look at me, like she could feel the heat on me, feel it coming off me. Her head swung back towards Vic. 'Why don't you tell her about Regina,' she said, voice thick.

Regina.

He looked over at her, lifting his eyebrows. 'Regina who?'

She smiled nastily. 'Regina the furrier.'

'You knew Regina?' I said, my voice quavering in spite of myself.

'Sure,' he said, shoving his hands in his pockets. 'She made the rounds. We've yapped on occasion.'

'I'd say so. You were flopping at her apartment until a few months back.'

'What does this mean?' I said, my voice trailing off.

'It means the whole setup was a setup,' she said. 'This chiseler got Regina to make nice with you.'

'To take her share of the Dutton job?' I asked, feeling a cold wetness at my temples, on my palms.

'And to get in with you, Little Miss Muffet,' she said, and I couldn't look at her because I knew it was true. I looked at him instead, and it got my blood up. It got some steel in my bones to see him so bare. *How many ways can you play the sap?* I asked myself. *You played them all.*

'You been working me from the start?' I said, cold as she taught me.

128

'I never played a dame,' he said, shaking his head, backing up a little. 'There's no dividend in it. Not even the ones with bank accounts of their own. They all got some fella behind the scenes ready to make trouble. Sugar daddies, lawyers, private bankers, vag husbands back in town.' He was talking way too much. It was all laying out there now, splayed out.

'So where's Regina now? What, she's gone home crying to Ma?'

'Buried under two feet of lime for all I know,' he said, and the hardness hit me like a sucker punch. 'But not from me,' he added. 'She was spreading her sweet butter all over town. Sure, I heard about the stones, but I wasn't in on that and I sure as hell would've stopped her from jawing about it door to door, flashing her new belly button emerald to every fast-money boy on the strip.'

'That's bunk,' she said, walking toward him slowly. 'And you know it. She took her shot because she'd borrowed heavy to cover *your* debts and then she was in deep with the sharks herself. So she got a nice haul from the jewelry deal, but before she could pay off her cuff, you'd taken her honey pot for yourself and dumped it all on another chalk bet at the track.'

He smiled again, but it was a sickly smile, toothless, like the broken men who played Texas twist for bottles of applejack in the lowest sawdust joints in the lowest part of town.

'She had to pull a Houdini,' she went on, 'or they'd have strung her up. So you figured you'd move on to the bigger catch. The one you'd had your eye on all along. That's why you kept your pretty face out of the rock heist. You were saving your grand entrance for my girl. You knew she'd have sweeter candy for you than little Regina ever could.'

'Ha. I should be so slick,' he said, looking over at me, rolling on the balls of his feet like a kid trying to bluff at the blackboard. 'I'm a bettor, and a bad one. I'm no hustler. Hell, angel face over there knows, I can't plan fifteen minutes ahead.'

'Lucky for you, you don't have to,' she said, and I saw the hand go into her purse. And I knew what was coming. And I didn't know if I cared. I didn't know anything. My hand rose slightly at my side as if to say something, stop something. But it all felt hollow. I didn't feel a thing.

Not even when I saw the revolver in her silver-gloved hands.

'Hey, look,' he said, backing away lifting his arms up at his sides like an old pro. 'Let's jaw this around a bit. What do you want, the scratch? Sure, I lost it, but I can win it back. Give me a day, two tops.'

Beads of sweat began popping on his brow. Oh, Vic. But I felt nothing, not even satisfaction.

'You think we want your sad little chump change,' she said and my eyes were on the gold grips of the revolver.

'That's going to be loud,' I found myself saying.

'It's not a blaster,' she said matter-of-factly, without even looking at me. 'Besides, you think anyone around here cares? There'll be a parade.'

He was backing up. I wondered if he had a gun. I'd never seen him with one. If he'd had one, he'd probably hocked it for another round of blackjack. I eyed his open suit jacket but saw nothing. Then, as his arm turned, I spotted the flash of a blade under his shirt cuff. So he was dumb but not that dumb. He'd been ready for something, someone. But who did he think he was dealing with that a knife was going to save him?

'You're going to shoot me because she's a liar and a tramp,' he suddenly barked, nodding toward me, his face greenish, gleaming with fear. 'How's that work?'

It was a mistake. He couldn't know it, but it was a mistake. I saw the heat rise back up in her. It was visible. He couldn't have known, but there it was.

'You think you can talk that way, think you can manhandle my girl, knock her around, put the scare in her, beat her until she ponies up for you? Bruise her fine flesh?' Her chignon came loose, that satiny auburn hair tumbling. 'Well, that's my flesh you're marking, little boy.'

'Manhandle? Pony up?' He looked over at me, then back at her. 'Is that what she told you—'

'He's got a knife,' I blurted out, before he could go on. Sure, I did. Who'd turned me out? She'd take me with her to the end, not just to the nearest strip of silk. Besides, how did I know that gun wouldn't turn on me?

Before he could speak, I heard a strange wail come from her and saw the silver-gloved fingers squeeze and the two shots in fast succession.

They felt like the loudest noises I'd ever heard, booming in my ears.

I looked over at him and there was a quick, hot splatter of blood from his face.

No, his jaw. She'd hit him in the jaw. He began to lean forward and I saw the other shot had gotten him in the gut, but barely.

Had she tried to kill him and missed? At just ten feet away?

He started lurching toward her, hand under his chin, flaps of skin and muscle hanging from where his lower jaw had been.

In spite of everything, his eyes were shining and I thought I could see the corners of his mouth rising, like he was smiling at his luck. Like he would have been smiling if he could have, if his smile hadn't been half torn away. Maybe under all the pulp, he was smiling.

Either way, he was going for the gun and everything went so fast and the next thing I knew they were intertwined, he was grabbing her legs as he collapsed, and the gun went flying, landed in the far corner of the room, then slid across the bare floor and into the bedroom.

'Get it. Get the goddamned gun,' she was growling as he writhed on the floor, clinging at her, dragging her down.

I saw the knife slip from his sleeve, saw its flash. He couldn't reach for it, she was on him, the heel of her hand wedged in his gut wound, twisting. But I wanted that knife. I didn't want that knife in anyone else's hands.

Dropping to my knees, I made a lunge for it as it lay several inches from Vic's shaking fingertips.

I meant only to take it out of both of their grasps. That was all I wanted. To get it out of reach. But before I knew what I was doing I was looking at his outstretched hand, still reaching for it as he wrestled with her. His hand was wriggling and I saw his eyes dart over toward me, *asking me something, asking me for something. And then. And then.*

I raised the knife and plunged it down through the center of his hand and into the wooden floor. The sound he made was not a cry or a shout but a sad little wheeze, soft and despondent.

Rising to my feet, I scrambled across the room for the gun. I didn't know what I was going to do with it, but I was going to get it.

It was on the floor of the bedroom and a bullet had popped out and rolled. I grabbed that too, shoving it back in the chamber as I ran back into the living room.

I couldn't have been gone more than ten seconds, five maybe.

But the wrestling match had ended. She was on top of him, legs astride. I saw the knife standing up, wedged into the floor, pinning his hand down, and she had the letter opener out. It was out and raised above her head.

'I have the gun. I have the gun,' I shouted.

Her head darted around to look at me. *Her eyes, were they red?*

And a low, ugly whisper: 'I don't want the gun.'

I thought she was just going to finish him off, don't you see? Yeah, that was bad too, but he wasn't going to make it anyhow, his face falling off, a bullet rolling around in his gut. I thought she was just going to finish the job, a deep, clean jag across the throat without the noise of another gunshot. Maybe the opener's point was sharp enough. Maybe she could make it quick.

But there was something wrong. She was lifting her arms in those strange, jerking moves, like she was on strings and when I saw the pointy tip ... and then it went down and up and down and up in jittering motions, like an old movie reel jumping and rocking. And the blood kept spinning up like a Tilt-A-Whirl and it was spraying her face and her hair and I saw that she'd slipped off her mask, finally, and here was her heat but look what kind of heat it was.

Her gloves soaked through red, pooling in her fingertips. She peeled them off and they fell like swollen petals in a pile beside her and still she didn't stop. She couldn't stop. I saw that. She'd never stop.

I tossed the gun and grabbed her under her arms and pulled as hard as I could, fighting her strength. I think now that it was the first time I'd ever touched her, she who'd put her hand on me countless times, adjusting my clothes, smoothing my hair, straightening my seams, grooming me, making me…

I lifted her to her feet. Her arms, her hands, her whole torso was shaking. We both nearly slipped on the slick floor.

The letter opener was in her hand, her grip so tight her fingers had slipped and I could see its blade pressed in her palm. Still standing behind her, I uncurled her fingers from it one by one until it dropped to the floor with a clatter.

'Well, that's done,' she muttered, breathless. She was looking down. I couldn't look down. But I could smell the horrible sweetness and could feel it.

I stepped back and bent down to pick up the gun, and as I did, I saw her silver stiletto pull back right beside Vic's head, then kick forward, tugging the last strands of muscle loose and sending the jaw bone skimming across the floor towards me.

'Don't worry,' she said, turning towards me, cool as ever. 'We'll find someone else for you to fuck.'

We might have been standing there thirty seconds or thirty years. She was figuring things, you could see her running it down in her head. And her chest was heaving, and she was giving off waves of heat. She was deciding what to do, how to fix it. I was watching her, wondering how it happened, wondering how she'd lost it all.

The front of her sharkskin suit steeped in blood, her stockings drenched red along the shin bones, her hair spattered with it. Worst of all was her face. I kept thinking of those pictures of South Seas headhunters in *Weird Tales*. When I was a kid, I'd look at those pictures for hours, my fingers pressed on the pages, on the fearsome *mandaus* they brandished, hair teeth and claws rising from the hilts. I'd have nightmares they were coming for me, crossing oceans and continents for fair-faced little girls to behead, to roast on spits over the fire. That's what she looked like, she looked like one of those Dyak warriors, her face red and raw, streaked and spangled.

Gloria, all those stories about you were true. And they weren't half as dark as this.

As we stood there, I knew I wasn't going to be able to say a word. I couldn't imagine what I could say. I wasn't looking at the body in the corner, and I couldn't bear to look her in the face. I stared at the floor.

Finally, she spoke. 'It's going to work like this,' she said. 'You're taking the El Dorado. You're going to do three things. Are you ready? Are you with me? Pull it together, kid.'

I forced myself to meet her gaze, but she couldn't make me focus my eyes. Instead, I looked at a blur of red, red hair, red face, red lips, snaky tongue.

'What...' I whispered. If I was going to get through this, I needed cool Gloria back, in her cool white suits, her precise French twists, her powdered face, textureless, planar, marble.

'Don't turn greenhorn on me now,' she said, facing me. 'Listen up. I want you to take the gun and the letter opener. I want you to drop the gun in the sewer drain, but drive at least five miles from town. By the paper mill. Got it? Then drive over by the loading docks and drop the letter opener in the water.

'I'm hoping I don't need to tell you to make sure no one sees you. Do whatever you have to do to dodge any eyes. Then drive to your place, it's closer, and pick me up a coat, something long, your trench coat. And a bag. A shopping bag. I can't walk out of here with this butcher's apron on. You get it, baby? You get it?'

She grabbed my chin in her hand. It was wet and she wanted it on me. She wanted his blood on me. She curled her fingers so high up my chin they touched the bottom of my lips. The wet touched my lips and lingered there.

'You're going to do it and you're going to do it smart. And don't even think of going Pollyanna on me,' she muttered. 'That knife didn't get there by itself.'

We both turned and looked at Vic's knife poised there, straight in the air. Still in his hand. Still in Vic's hand. Had I done that?

Looking at it got my head on straight again, knocked the horror out of my bones and reminded me of the stakes here, for us

139

and for me. Reminded me of the world beyond that room, a world larger than all this, with rules, laws, machines of its own that didn't care about my dread, about what I had going on inside me, about the ugly red haze stuck in my head.

Then, hearing her breathing next to me, smelling it, and smelling the desperation on her, I realized I had to do something. I had to show her I wasn't going soft. If she thought I was going soft, there was no telling what she'd do.

I walked over, leaned down, and yanked the knife out. I made sure I didn't even twitch when the body jolted with the motion.

Holding up the knife, I said, 'Guess I'll toss this while I'm at it.'

She looked at me, her right hand dangling at her side. I could feel the blood on my chin, along my jawline where that hand had been.

'Guess you'd better,' she said.

I walked, slow as she ever did, to where my handbag lay and kneeled down for it, tossing the knife inside. Still kneeling, I arced my arm in a wide circle, sweeping the gun and the letter opener into the bag as well. Then I rose and pulled out a handkerchief and my compact. Looking straight into the mirror, straight at my face, batter white except for the two thick, gruesome red streaks down either side of my mouth, I ran the handkerchief over my chin, dainty as a society lady at a dinner party.

'I'll be back in thirty minutes,' I said, tucking the purse under my arm, twisting on my heels, and walking out.

Out on the street, I breathed the misty air as deep as I could. After that small space, hot, wet, and close, like the inside of something slowly constricting, I was grateful for the chill in the air, the strangely clean smell of exhaust fumes, factory grit, the whole steel and concrete feel.

In the car, I kept the windows rolled all the way down even though the night was raw. I ignored the stench still in my nostrils. I ignored the rearview mirror, didn't want to see my face. There was a sound in my head that I wanted to drown out. There was a sound that was knocking around up there. It was the sound of his shoe hitting the radiator again and again with each swing of her arm, each time she brought that brass blade down. Over and over and over and I was standing there. And I was watching and his torso was spraying blood like an atom-

141

izer. And I was glad I was standing behind her so I couldn't see his face, or hers.

When I was back at his building, my errands done, I stopped myself before going inside. The thought of going in that room again. The thought of what she might be like now. But the only other choice was to skip town and never come back. She had my number now. We were bound together. It had happened that fast and now there was no way out.

I knocked at his door and didn't hear anything. But I could feel her on the other side of the door. She was silent, but I tell you I could feel her there. The charge coming off her, and the fear in her too, and I don't know which was more surprising.

I leaned forward and whispered, barely a whisper, 'It's me.'

The door opened slowly and I slipped in, my herringbone trench over my arm. She shut the door fast behind me. I saw she'd washed her face, fixed her hair, erased everything from the neck up, and it was all smooth again. Smooth like a mannequin. But if you looked close enough, you could still see gritty specks in her hair. I could see them.

She began unbuttoning her jacket, its

browning blood, its awfulness. She peeled it off. I averted my eyes as I heard her unzip the skirt, peel off the stockings, which made a sucking noise, the nylon weighted with rusting blood. I didn't want to see any more.

'Hand it to me,' she demanded and I had to look as I tossed the coat to her. I had to look at her. She was wearing a full slip and the blood had seeped through to the delicate silk to her white, white skin, like pearly wax.

'The bag.'

I handed her the shopping bag I'd brought and she dropped her things in it.

'Okay,' she said, pulling the coat on, tying the sash tightly around her waist, then raising the collar until it stood crisply, chicly, framing her cheekbones. With the Monroe's Fine Clothes bag dangling from her wrist, she might as well have been the mayor's wife on her way to high tea and cucumber sandwiches.

'So what are we doing now?' I asked, nodding toward the bloody corner.

'Don't worry about that.'

'We're just leaving it?' I said, trying to keep my voice low but feeling a growing panic. 'What about John Law?'

'What about it? Since when have you been

worried about them?'

I looked at her, feeling that pinching feeling in my head again. 'Since when?' I asked, trying to keep the hysteria out of my voice. 'Since that,' I said, pointing at the corner. 'Since *that*.'

'Don't worry, honey,' she repeated, tucking one last stray wisp of hair into place. 'It's all taken care of.'

'What do you mean,' I said, my voice turning queer. I wondered for a scary second if she'd lost her mind, if she'd somehow forgotten everything, wiped it as clean as her blank face.

'The Mounties'll just think Mackey finally took his due.'

'Gloria,' I said. 'The body. Mackey's boys don't ... do those things. They don't do it like that. That way. They don't...' I paused.

She was almost smiling and it sent a hard blast of cold up my spine.

'Gloria, when they see the body...'

She shrugged. 'There isn't going to be a body to see.'

'Gloria, you don't mean for us to get rid of it?'

'We don't do that sort of job,' she said, as if her hands hadn't been drenched in hot blood a half hour before. 'I called Mackey.

He's sending his hard boys over. They're taking care of it.'

'You called... But why would they do that for you?'

'Because I'm paying off this pantywaist's vig,' she said, jabbing her thumb toward the corner of the room as though Vic were there to listen, to hear the distaste in her voice.

'My God, Gloria, you're paying off thirty Gs?'

She looked at me for a second and the whisper of a smile slanted across her lips. 'Thirty? Honey, Vic Riordan owed Mackey two grand even.'

Here was the ultimate sucker punch. One last parting gift from Vic, from beyond the grave. 'Are you sure?' I tried, my mouth dry.

'Sure as summer rain, baby. You think they'd've given that cheapjack a leash so long? He owed that much, he'd've been hanging by his toes a month ago.'

'Right,' I said. What could I say, after all.

She walked over to the light switch and turned it off and on again. 'That's their signal to come up. Then we can beat it.'

'Okay,' I said. 'But what did you tell Mackey?'

'I told him we know how to take care of business.'

A few minutes later, two boys with ham-hock upper arms strolled in the door. One carried a long canvas bag, like the kind my old man had from his army days.

'Holy Christ,' the one with the bag said, lifting his cap off his forehead as he walked over to where the body lay.

'How tall you think he is?' the other muttered, rubbing his face tiredly. 'I don't think we'll need the lye.'

'The bathtub's that way,' Gloria said. 'And you saw the back entrance in the alley, right?'

'Yeah,' the first one said, still looking at the body. He couldn't take his eyes off it. Neither of them could. 'We saw it.'

'Okay,' she said, cocking her head toward me. 'Let's blow.'

I looked over at her and there was something in her face that was almost worse than anything that had come before. Almost worse than what that white mask concealed. It was satisfaction. It was satisfaction stone-cut into her face, into the corners of her mouth, which lifted just high enough to approach a smile. It was the ugliest thing I'd seen all night. The ugliest thing I'd ever seen, sure.

'Yeah,' I managed. 'Let's blow.'

146

We drove back to her place. She wanted me to stay with her. She said it was a precaution, that in case there were complications we should be ready at a moment's notice. But I knew the real reason. She thought I might skip or worse. She wanted a close watch on me. She wasn't going to take her eyes off me.

I spent the night on her sofa, tangled up in an oversize satin tufted bedspread, staring out into the dark of the room, eyes on her half-open bedroom door.

I felt bone tired but years away from real sleep. And I couldn't get my heart to stop jackhammering. There was no sound coming from her room and her light was off, but I couldn't imagine how she could be sleeping either. All I could think about was the things I'd seen that night. All I could think about was what I'd let loose. I'd been rooked by Vic, that was true, but it was penny-ante stuff in the big picture. I started to wonder what she would have done if she'd known everything. If she'd known I wasn't a knocked-around girlfriend beaten into giving up the goods for her man. What

147

would she have done if she knew I was in the center of the whole setup?

Then I thought maybe she did know but didn't want to look at it. Maybe she did know but there's all kinds of lies you tell yourself when you want to. Like the lie I was telling myself about what I'd done that night. The lie that said I did what I had to. I had no choice.

But, I reminded myself, there was Vic fixing me from the start, in cahoots with the furrier, watching me and waiting for me, to ride me to fat city, a place Vic had to know he'd never stay for long, always one bet away from the skids. Always counting seconds to his next big loss, and now he'd hit this last one.

Who was I to feel a heart-tug about his sayonara? He'd played me like easy pickings. I wasn't about to cry into my pillow for him.

I'd been lying there for an hour or more, drifting in and out of near-sleep, of bad dreams, of cannibals with sharpened teeth, with necklaces made of bone, with shrunken heads hanging by long tails of hair from their raised hands.

I can't be sure I was really awake, it's true. But I tell you, my eyelids weren't all the way closed and through my lashes, even in the blue-dark of the room, I could see her standing there. Standing at the foot of the sofa in her ermine-colored robe looking at me. Too dark to see her face (there was no face, just a black maw), but it was her. Light from the streetlamp shot through her hair.

She was standing there and for a minute I thought, *This is it.* She'd been waiting for me to fall asleep and now she was going to finish me off. Why wouldn't she? Once she stepped back, she had to realize, like I did, that we were bound now and she couldn't let there be anyone out there who had something on her. And worse still, she couldn't let there be somebody out there who'd seen the dark thing behind her eyes, the dark thing crawling under her skin. I'd seen it. I'd seen it.

But she didn't move and I didn't move. And then, finally, she seemed to recede back into the darkness and I closed my eyes tighter and I almost started praying. Honest. I almost started praying like I haven't done since my communion, since I started filling out, since my old man stopped sitting on the edge of the bed when he said good night.

In the morning, she came out of her bedroom dressed to the nines, from her tucked satin hat to her bleach-white gloves to the gardenia on her collar.

'I've got the rounds to do,' she said. 'I'll be gone all day. You can wear this.' She handed me a mint-colored day suit on a hanger. 'It'll be long on you, but it'll be all right for today. I'll have some of your things sent here.'

I stopped myself from asking how long she saw this new living arrangement lasting.

In the bathroom, I put the suit on, the smell of her perfume woven in it, choking in my throat as I lifted it over my head. I didn't look in the mirror.

When I walked out, she walked towards me, checking how low the hem fell and finally approving. 'It'll do. I'll drop you off at your car. While I'm gone, you'll be taking care of this.' She handed me a crisp envelope, thick with bills.

'What am I doing with that?' I said.

'Taking it to the Venetian Gardens,' she said. 'But slather on some more paint before you go. You still look like something hanging in a meat market.'

'I'm the one making the drop to Mackey?' I said, resisting the urge to touch my face.

'Why not? It's your boyfriend's tab. Isn't that fair play?' She ran her hand briskly across a faint wrinkle on her seersucker skirt.

'What if he asks me questions? What am I supposed to say?' It was slowly beginning to hit me. I'd been too crazy the night before to really see things. Now, in the glare of daylight, the way she'd cleaned up no longer looked so clean. It looked shoddy, desperate. One of the big rules was never to let anyone have something on you, the way we had something on each other now. But there'd been no avoiding that. What we could've avoided was Mackey having something on us. What'd stop him from using it?

'If he braces you, just give him your toothiest smile. Shrug your shoulders and play the hip-grinding vestal. It's an act you got down.'

'What does that mean?'

She threw me my purse. 'It means you're a long way from pro, honey, but you sure know how to play both sides to your advantage.'

The minute I was in my car, or at least the car that she allowed me to use, I felt my foot twitching over the gas, ready to hit the interstate and hightail it out of town for good. I could leave the state, drive clear across to Saint Louis, Memphis, Denver, Colorado. So far she'd never find me. Change my name. Go back to school. Take dictation in a big office of actuaries or CPAs or junior executives in dark flannel suits with leather briefcases who took commuter trains that delivered them to warm-faced wives in oven mitts. And maybe someday I'd be one of those warm-faced wives in oven mitts, with red-cheeked Tommy and cork-screw-curled Debbie nestling into my skirts.

I could have that.

I could have that.

Just step harder on the gas. Turn the wheel hard at the next left and be on the interstate and never look back.

But she would find me.

She would find me.

Look at the heat in her when she's double-crossed, when she's betrayed. How could she not find me?

She'd track me down and string me up by the hair and slice me up the middle, and make Tommy and Debbie watch. She knew how to end things. She knew how to make it so you'd never forget. Never shake the sight of her in full dark bloom.

She was an artist.

The Venetian Gardens was jammed in the center of the ritz district that ran along the western ridge of town. Outside was a stone façade and a fountain that gushed out cascades of gold-flecked water from a big copper Neptune. Inside, the place was decked out with black and gold columns, gold-dust glass candelabras, and gold-marbled mirrors from wall to ceiling. To get to the main dining room you had to walk across a replica marble Bridge of Sighs. In the evening all these fireworks probably made you feel like Italian royalty, but by daylight it hurt your eyes.

I walked straight back to the kitchen, where I found the guy with the cap from the night before. Seeing him reminded me of everything all at once, but I tried to steel myself from it. I didn't want him to see it on me. I thought about how he'd spent his night – had he been shovel-to-dirt out on the far end of town or tying cement bags to Vic's ankles for a quick drive to the waterfront?

As I approached him, he was pawing through a large crate he'd propped up on the counter, dozens of Waterford crystal figurines, ring holders and drooping angels, seahorses and conch shells, picking each one up and brushing off the sawdust with surprising care. When he saw me, I thought he might drop one.

'Is the big man around?' I asked.

'Yeah,' he said slowly, putting the crystal bunny-with-egg back in the box and closing it. 'I'll tell him you're here.' He hesitated, and I thought he might say something.

'Look, I'm in a hurry,' I said.

He looked at me for a second longer, lifting his cap above his eyes, like he'd done the night before.

'If you don't mind my asking,' he said, 'how does a little cupcake like you get her lily whites stuck in something like that? Like last night? You should be going to dances.' He tilted his head, then added, a soft, brotherly burr in his voice, 'You should be dancing with boys.'

What he said, it rubbed me wrong. I knew I should feel relieved that he thought I was some poor kid along for the ride. But I didn't. The fear that had been quaking through me for ten hours gave over to something hard, spiky, still.

'My lily whites,' I said, raising my gloved fingers, 'have been in far worse than that, chump.' I don't know where it came from, but there I was, mouthing off like nothing had happened. I was just a hard girl making her rounds.

I walked over and picked up a crystal Cross-of-the-Faithful and turned it in my hand. 'And I don't dance for anybody,' I added, echoing something she'd once said. Hadn't she? I couldn't keep track anymore. I couldn't keep track.

Before I could get to Amos Mackey himself, I had to talk to one of his suits, a greasy-faced fella with thick eyebrows and French cuffs and an unclean air about him. He looked like he'd just graduated one step above muscle but hadn't figured out yet how to wear the new wardrobe. He was standing in front of the leather-padded office door like a sentinel.

'Look,' I said. 'I'm just delivering something. Mr. Mackey's expecting it. But I need to make sure he gets it.'

He hooked his thumbs in his vest and looked at me. 'You're Gloria Denton's girl?'

'Yeah.'

'That's all you needed to say, baby,' he said, real sing-songy 'He's expecting you.' He moved aside, but as he did he gave me a quick up-and-down look and I didn't like it. It was a knowing look and it made me feel like my slip was showing. What had this goon

155

heard, and if a goon like this knew something, who knew how many goons like him might know?

Trying to shake it off, I walked into the office, which was nearly the size of the main dining room, with heavy tapestries hanging from the ceiling and more gold columns built into the walls. I half expected a roaring fireplace in the corner.

Mackey was on the phone, a big brass and marble number. He was speaking softly into the receiver with his eyes on me.

I stood before him, not bothering to sink into the massive leather chair in front of his desk.

He spoke a few more words, in low tones, into the receiver, then hung up.

I'd never seen him up close before, and boy, was he a groomed and fragrant figure, as if a hundred hands had been on him already that day. Freshly barbered and shaved, smelling of fine cologne, skin pink and smooth like a cherub's, he sure didn't look like the fellows I usually delivered to, all of whom had the gray sheen of men who'd never seen sunlight, who spent their whole lives in dim-lit casinos, absorbing smoke and midshelf liquor.

'So Miss Denton didn't come herself,' he said.

'No, she sent me instead.'

He nodded. 'Why don't you have a seat?'

'That's all right,' I said. I didn't want to be there any longer than I had to. I kept thinking about what he had on us, on me. With a word to our bosses, those men on Gloria's phone, the ones whose ringed hands everything that passed through mine landed in, we could suddenly become not worth the trouble. Wasn't that right? And wouldn't they be none too happy that we'd gone to this local overseer and not them for help?

'I'm just dropping this off,' I said, holding the envelope out towards him. He looked at it without moving.

'We met before,' he said.

'I don't think so,' I replied, even as I remembered our exchange months before at the While-a-Way Cocktail Lounge, after my Gloria routine, my tough-guy number with the owner. *'I like it,' he'd said, with a ghost of a smile. 'I like it.'*

'Well, not formally. But I wouldn't forget you,' he said, but without a flicker of flirtation in his voice. It was serene, relaxed. 'You know, you could sit down. We could talk over some things. We might have some topics of mutual interest, if you were so inclined.'

The patter was smooth, sticky, tupelo

honey. But you could feel there was something solid behind it, like oak. Like he was one of those sober-faced men behind the big desks in the movies. The ones who played the judges or bank presidents or Abraham Lincoln. I could see what people meant when they said he wasn't long for shark business. That was a way to fill coffers in the first stretch. The things I'd heard about him, they were making sense.

But if so, he was taking quite a risk still dipping his cashmere toe into mop-ups like last night. He must've seen a major rake-off to take that chance. What was the payoff?

'I really have to get back.' I said.

He was looking up at me, eyes squinting slightly, looking so closely I almost backed up a step. 'I don't want to keep you,' he said. 'But it's a standing offer.'

He picked up the phone as if to make another call. I set the envelope down on his desk.

'So long, Mr. Mackey, I said, as softly as him. Something about him called for hushed tones and meaningful stares and polite nods, followed by brief phone calls where everything is taken care of without anyone ever raising a voice.

'Give my regards to Miss Denton,' he said.

'And tell her to come here to dine. I promise her the white-glove treatment.'

'Right,' I said, trying to read him. Trying and failing. You can't read a top dog's face. That's why they're top dog.

After I closed the door behind me, I stood there. Mackey's goon was watching me, picking his nails with a crystal-handled nail file. He smiled, gums gleaming.

I walked past him without saying anything. I wanted to get out of there. I wanted to get out of everywhere, all these places and their back rooms and back offices and back alleys. All these whispers and winks and knowing glances and everybody knowing, or maybe knowing, everything you'd done, everything you were. I didn't want them to know what I was.

On the way back to her place, I stopped and picked up an afternoon paper. I'd been avoiding it. Hadn't glanced at the morning edition, didn't want to see if anything was in there. Sitting in my car, I read the news, local news, and crime beat sections. Not a word about Vic. Not that there should be.

It struck me suddenly. How long could a guy like that go missing before someone reported him missing? Days, months, more?

Besides his girlfriend and his shark, who would notice?

That was when I started to cry. But it was only a few seconds. It was fast and then it was done. I wouldn't even tell you, but it happened. I was weak and I cried in three fast, soundless jags and then I stopped, powdered my face, and started the car again. I tossed the newspaper out the window the minute I hit the boulevard.

Oh, Vic, remember when you came home with those miniature roulette wheels you'd pinched from the casino promotion office? You'd passed me the key to your place earlier that night and you came in late, you were tight from whiskey sours and you came in and I was in your bed, not a stitch on like you liked it and you were so lit you'd boosted a whole box of those novelty miniature roulette wheels. Remember how you laid me down and set one on my belly and spun it? How you blew on it to make it spin? Remember that? You said I was lucky for you, that it was only straight-up bets for you and me. But I knew. I knew what you really had in mind was a skin game. That's what you had in mind all along, even as you spun the roulette wheel, chin resting on my stomach, razor bristle on my skin. The whirring of the wheel.

160

That night, I waited for her in that gloomy chromium-trimmed apartment of hers. I mixed myself seven and sevens, slinking around the place, running my fingertips over the plush surfaces, the high-class statuary, the *objets*, than what they called them in the deep-pocket stores that sold them to her.

By the second drink, the slinking had turned to sauntering. The way the whiskey was tingling behind my eyes, I started to get ideas. Who did she think she was anyway, putting us both in the bull's eye? And now she thought she could keep me prisoner here, locked up in her silver-decked tower, sent out only at her pleasure?

By the third drink, though, the swagger started to wane. The panicky feeling from earlier in the day was coming back. Everywhere I turned I thought of things we'd forgotten to do, things that could trap us. When I looked at the satin moire drapes on her windows, I thought about the half-drawn blinds in Vic's apartment. What if someone had seen us through the window? When I leaned against the far wall and could hear a neighbor's warbling radio, I thought about the two gunshots, the struggle on the floor. Anyone could have heard and it would be over for us.

And Mackey. If Mackey was as big as his spread looked, as his spending looked, building new restaurants every week and, if the rumblings about him turned out to be true, buying acres and acres of land on the waterfront for a rumored new high-class racetrack, buying interests in welterweights, in shipping companies, in importing companies with fat government contracts – if he were doing half these thing, he could be a very dangerous man. How could we be sure what he'd do, what his motives might be?

So I poured myself one more drink, a short one. And as the booze kicked in, I drummed up some of the bluster again. Before I knew it, I was sashaying around her bedroom, deep into her treasure chest of jewels, dangling her diamond fan earrings, her South Sea pearl drops from my ears, donning the favored aquamarine and citrine fringe necklace, then the diamond *sautoir*, followed by the angel-skin coral choker.

As I pulled each piece out, expecting to find anything from the Hope diamond to a necklace made of human tongues, I felt tougher and tougher. A few months before I wouldn't have dared to set foot in her bedroom without permission, but now everything had changed. She'd shown me something and everything had changed.

Not that I was a fool, not that kind of fool at least. I returned each piece to its place, nestled in individual fabric pouches.

After I'd made my way through the sparkly wampum, though, I was primed for more. My balance slightly off from the last drink, my heel catching in the thick carpet, I tripped over to her long-mirrored, walk-in closet and waded through its soft treasures. Digging my hands deeper and deeper, through the brocades, bouclé, and nubby wool, I felt my fingers touch something slippery and familiar. A sickly feeling rushed through me, wiping out all four drinks in an instant.

Quickly, I shoved everything along the closet rod to get a look, hoping it was a mistake, that I was just tight. But sure enough, there it was, at the far, far end of the closet, almost completely concealed by a peacock-green beaded evening coat.

The red dress I'd worn the night before, through it all. Through everything. The dress I'd finally peeled off at three A.M., shivering and shaken to the core. She'd asked me to hand it to her through the partially open bathroom door. She was going to take it down to the incinerator, along with her own suit, brittle brown from collar to knee. She'd draped it over her arm. Hadn't I seen her walk out of the apartment with them?

But no, there it was hanging in the far back corner of her closet, the jeweled front tugging down the padded hanger. There it was with the fresh rip in the back slit from one of the many times I'd hit the floor. I pulled it out and held it up to the smoked glass sconce, looking frantically for any stains. And there were stains. A rusty scatter along the bottom hem, just visible against the red. A plum-sized smear just under the neckline. I remembered that one. *Pulling her back against me, against my chest, pulling her off with all I had in me. I did do that, Vic. I didn't let it go on forever. She might have gone on forever. I did do that, Vic.*

So here it was. She was holding this. She was holding this to have something on me. She was biding her time, waiting to see if she'd need to use it. Or planning on using it, the time just hadn't come yet.

I probably should have stuffed the thing in a

grocery bag first, but it felt like there was no time at all. Dress wrapped around my fists and forearms, nearly sliding from my grasp like some enormous tongue, I tore down the back stairway's seven flights.

In the bleach-soaked basement, it took me a long, sweaty minute and a half to find the incinerator hatch. Pushing my hair out of my eyes, off my wet forehead, I jerked open the heavy door and tossed the dress in, letting the blast hit me square in the face, hearing the awful red thing sizzling for a second then disappearing into flames. I slammed the trap shut without a second glance.

Who did she think she was making? She'd taught me herself and she thought I'd roll over so easy?

'So how'd the drop-off go?' she asked when she finally got home, near one o'clock. 'Mackey catechize you?'

'No,' I said, thinking hard. Thinking about what I was going to say to her and which chips I'd hold on to.

'Did he pull anything raw?'

I leaned back, surprised. 'Raw? No. Why?'

She shrugged, unpinning her hat. 'I kinda had an idea he might like a touch of your downy silks.'

'Is that why you sent me?'

She didn't respond. Instead, she leaned over me, turning my face from one side to the other, appraising my wounds, every ding and purple dent. 'A few more days, chickie baby, and you'll be back in the saddle.'

'Was that why you sent me?' I tried again.

She sighed shallowly, then slowly began loosening her hair from a handful of tight bobby pins. 'I got the impression, nothing to put my finger on, that Mackey had been eyeing you, had an itch for you. Thought it might make him less inclined to stronghand us. Only looking out for us both, kid.'

I kept my eyes fixed on the wall behind her, on the scalloped shelf with the tall marble gazelle on it. If I looked at her, I'd lose my guts.

I forced the words out of my mouth. 'Gloria, everyone there was looking at me like they knew. How can you think we're not getting collared for this?'

She ran a pair of fingers through her hair, stretching out each auburn twist, almost with a languor. I couldn't get a rise out of her. Who would've believed she'd been breathing fire twenty-four hours before?

'Listen, kid,' she said, 'as much as Amos

166

Mackey's got on us, we've got a dozen more tales to tell on him. As a for-instance, you think he wants the gendarmes to get wise to the five little Indians he's got buried in the wine cellar of Amos's Italian Grotto? I know everything there is to know about each one of those clips. He's got big ideas and he can't have anyone squawking about the things he did before he got those big ideas. Or the things he did to get the pot of honey to bankroll those big ideas.'

She was so confident, so cocksure. For a second, it worked on me. I started wondering if I was acting crazy like some hysterical girl. But then I reminded myself of the dress. If she was so confident, why keep a bargaining chip? I thought of that dress and everything started jumping in me. 'How about those errand boys from last night?' I said. 'Who knows who they'll tell?'

'Don't worry about the meat,' she said, watching me more closely now. Seeing something on me. 'They do as they're told. That's their job. Since when do you worry, anyway? Have I ever queered you before? Have I ever laid you open?'

'Yes, Gloria,' I said, my voice crackling, popping. I couldn't stop it. It was happening and I couldn't stop it. 'You have, Gloria.

Last night. You ruined everything, don't you see? You broke all your own rules. You said never to lose control. And you did. *You fucked up and we're both going to hang for it.*'

I thought, as I heard myself, as the terrible words came out of my mouth, I might turn to stone on the spot. But they were out there. They were out there and there was no taking them back.

'How many cocktails have you had anyway, dear heart?' she said, unbuttoning her cuffs but with her eyes on me. 'Been crying in your beer over your boyfriend?'

'Don't talk about him,' I blurted out. 'Don't you talk about him. Don't you dare.'

She tilted her head. 'So that's how it is, huh? A real love match and I tore you apart. Romeo and Juliet.'

'That's not how it is,' I bristled. After everything, I still found myself feeling insulted by what she'd said, what she was suggesting. 'I'm talking about business. About doing things smart. You broke all your own rules, Gloria. Anybody could've seen us, heard us. And you brought in other parties, parties we have no reason to trust. We're behind the eight ball because of you.'

She shook her head, still seemingly unfazed by the growing hysteria in my voice.

'This was your first time and I didn't prepare you,' she said, plain and even. 'I didn't set you up first. I should have, sure. But I needed you in the dark. Otherwise you would've given your boy a warning and he'd've copped a heel. The point is, there's nothing to worry about. This is how these things go.'

'Why didn't you just shoot him?' I said, the words slipping out of me in a trembling voice I didn't recognize. 'Why'd you have to do it to him that way? Like some...' I stopped myself. The whiteness in her face, the bullet-hole eyes. I stopped myself. Her eyes said to stop and I did.

There was a long, terrible silence. All the sound seemed sucked out of the world and I knew if I tried to open my mouth, tried to force a word up my throat, I would come up mute.

She rose and walked over to me, put one cold, gloveless hand on my shoulder. 'You've been through a lot, kid. You're going to be okay. If you think about it, you'll see how right I was. Because I'm taking care of us. I always take care of us.'

I went to sleep that night resolving to keep my mouth shut and my eyes open, biding my time. That was her best lesson to me, after all. If I was careful, maybe I'd see it coming, whatever it was.

If she saw the red dress was gone from her closet, she didn't say anything. I couldn't, see it on her, couldn't draw it out from the rest, from her whole cool, watchful way. I would stare at her face when she wasn't looking, and when she was, and I couldn't read a thing in it. In spite of everything, I envied her that. To wear that kind of face. It seemed like something impressive to me still. I couldn't shake that.

In the dream that kept coming, Vic was throwing down playing cards at the long green table, card after card skating through the air. He was watching me, not the cards, and he was smiling in that genial way of his, the way that said, Sure, I'm lying, baby, I'm always lying but just because I'm lying doesn't mean it isn't true too. And the cards fly up and I can't see his face for a second and when they flutter down again he looks different. He looks funny, like he's made of wood. I see the long line across his face, hooking from earlobe to earlobe like a ventriloquist's dummy, with the smile suspended from corner to corner. And then he throws the last card and he's still looking at me and he reaches up to this jaw and twists it first one way, then the other, with a sickening creak. He's holding it in his hands, that jaw, and I start to shut my eyes and he says something but I can't hear it and I look again and he's handing me the jaw across the table. He's handing it to me, and it's white and polished like a dog's picked-clean bone. I know he wants me to lift it up to my face to see if it fits, if it locks into place, but I'm afraid to. And his face is hanging half open, like it's come loose, but he's flipping those cards again. And smiling. Always smiling.

Three days went by and I was still sleeping on her sofa. I'd made some noise about going back to my place, but she'd just slanted her head at me and said, 'What's there that's not here, Kewpie doll?'

What could I say? Sure, I was scared of what she might do. But I was also being smart. I didn't want to seem too eager. I was working on my poker face. I was getting better at it. I'd spent all three days stuck in that marbled mausoleum of hers, thinking, thinking.

On the fourth day, I got my day pass. She

put the Pan-Cake on me herself. It took a half hour. She held my face in her silver-tipped hands and turned my chin this way and that way and I couldn't see what she was doing, but first it felt rough and gritty and eventually it was like she'd dipped my face in soft wax and carved out my features anew. Like wearing a face on top of my face.

She held her hand mirror to my face and I pretended to look but I didn't look.

She was giving me an easy ride that night. A few pickups to test the waters. I half wondered if she might follow me, but she ended up leaving first, saying she was going to check on three floating casinos on the river, a good sixty miles away. They weren't the money spinners they once were and the fellas upstairs were raising eyebrows.

I can't pretend it didn't feel good to be back in the mix, walking through my favorite velvet-walled, gold-telephone casinos. The shift bosses and the floor men and the regulars all wanted to buy me drinks, sorry to hear I'd been under the weather, tucked into bed for nearly a week with a bad case of the grippe.

I got to admit, though, when I hit the casino at Yin's Peking Palace, it was hard to keep up the dance. The minute I walked in, I remembered seeing Vic there for the first dine, winning and losing everything down to the lint in his pockets. But I tried to put it out of my head.

I let Larry, the manager, buy me a gin swizzle before I left.

'Word among the stickmen is it's been a slow week.'

'Not too,' Larry said, lighting a cigarette. 'Some of our regs haven't been in. There's a hot poker game over at the Mutual Federated Building on Sixth. Your bosses somehow got themselves the whole third floor, the old book depository. Vic Riordan hasn't darkened this doorstep all week, so I figured he was losing his shift there. But looks like not.'

I stared straight down into the glass and didn't even twitch. Something scraped inside me, a razory feeling up my back, but not for long. I wouldn't let it. I let the gin nip at me, licked my lower lip and raised my eyes and there was nothing there for Larry to see but my Pan-Cake and long lashes. I was proud I'd done it.

'Riordan?'

'Yeah, you know. Classic case: fish who thinks he's a shark,' he said, shaking his

head. 'But he ain't been swimming any-
where lately.'

'So maybe he finally hit it.'

'It ain't like that. He's not just in absentia.
There's more to it. The boys in blue were
sniffing around. We thought they came to
bust us. But I guess you know that's all covered,' he said, looking at me meaningfully.
Sure, it was true. We paid down every last
billy club that mattered in that precinct
every week.

'So what were they here for?'

'Seems they think Riordan's gone invisible.'

'Probably trying to beat a vig.'

'Maybe,' he said. 'But how's that get the
cops so interested?'

'So what kinds of questions were they
asking? Who he owed?' I said, treading carefully.

'Yeah, but not just that. They were bothering all my dealers, the cocktail waitresses,
everyone. Wanted to know who his friends
and not-so-friends were.'

'Huh,' I said.

That was all I said. But I knew where to go
next.

'Poor sap,' Larry said, sighing. 'He was a
lousy gambler and a lousy cheat. Once, he

174

even tried to roll shaved dice like we were running some two-bit crap game. But I still kinda liked the guy. You know?'

Sergeant Pulaski wasn't hard to find, parked in the corner pocket of Fahey's Bar on Sutton Street. Everyone knew: you buy him three short glasses at the nearest cop bar, he'd hand over his firstborn on a serving fork. That night, I was buying.

'I always liked you, kid,' he said, eyes shining over his rye. 'Always thought it was a crying shame such a sweet-faced filly got knotted up with such rotten trade.'

'You mean the trade that pays your mortgage, your bar tab, and your daughter's tuition at Saint Lucy's?'

'Yeah, they're the ones.' He grinned. 'Listen, I never said I was a clean liver. But I got rules to live by. As a for-instance, soft as I might find your skin, I'd never try to lay down my hand.' He took a quick nip and then his eyes turned still more soulful. 'I don't like to see it. You know, I got a daughter. At Saint Lucy's.'

'That so?'

'Dancing eye and freckles on the nose and never anything but grins for Pops. I tell you, I–'

'Sarge, I got this pin money in my purse and it's a little heavy,' I said, flashing him a twenty spot. 'I'm inclined to pass it over to our fine barkeep and call it a night. It's long past a Saint Lucy's girl's bedtime. What do you think? Can you help me with that?'

'My dear, I believe I can,' he said, straightening up on the bar stool.

'If only I could get a bedtime story first, to send me on my way.'

'Just call me Aesop. Pick your tale.'

'How 'bout the one about the card player, the wheel spinner, the bounder who went poof.'

'I just might know the magic man of whom you speak. No end yet, though there is a moral.'

'Okay, Sarge, lay it out for me.'

Pulaski shook his head. 'He's nowhere to be found, honey. His landlady called. Rolled it out like this: she hadn't seen hide nor hair of him for a couple days and wanted to see what's what. And then there was the little matter of a box spring of hers that had fallen into his possession. So she lets herself into the place and it's cleaned out. Then she remembers, all of a sudden like, she'd heard some funny noises coming from the joint a few days back.'

176

'What kinds of noises?'

'Bang-bang noises, what else?'

'Someone got tired of waiting to collect?'

'Could be. But those boys don't usually do such a full cleanup. Maybe the shylocks are getting more thorough. Or maybe they came meaning business, but our fella made it out the fire escape in time.'

I knew what she'd say. There's nothing to worry about, even less than before. The cops had been to Vic's and hadn't found a thing. What could be better?

But I didn't like it. There was something out there, something hanging in the air. I could feel it. It was like the stories you read when you're a kid, the Saturday matinees about the couple on the run, the tough guys pulling one last job. They all taught you how it would end up. You don't get out of this kind of snare so easy.

And sleeping on the sofa that night, thinking of how I might've played it different. How I might have played it smarter. If only Vic hadn't tagged me an easy mark. Didn't he know he could square-deal me, that I took him for what he was and he didn't need to do his dance for me? God help me, Vic, the things you could do to me, I would've given it over to you without all the pink lights and music, the whole carnival show you put on. Couldn't you feel it on me? Couldn't you see it in my eyes, behind the black enamel, metal lashes clicking shut? The things I did for you in there, when we were all alone, didn't they show you I didn't need to be played like a country girl in petticoats waiting for your traveling show? Didn't they show I was ready from the start?

It was close to midnight when she came home. Even before she turned on the floor lamp, I knew there was trouble. You could feel the nerves shooting off her.

'What's going on?' I asked, throwing the blanket off me.

'We're moving the body,' she said briskly, as if she'd just given me tomorrow's weather report.

'What? Why?' The cops. The cops must know. My heart was clanging like a trolley car as I jumped to my feet.

'Take it easy, kid,' she said, setting her purse, hat, and gloves down. 'I got shovels in the car. Just get dressed. Wear something discreet.'

I just stared at her. I half wondered if she expected me to pull out some kind of grave robber's getup. I wanted to laugh. And then

178

I did. I started to laugh. It was terrible laugh, like out of some kids' cartoon, loud and rhythmless and shrill.

The slap that came was hard. It radiated through me. And it was so fast that by the time I finished blinking, her hand was at her side again.

'Don't give me a hysterical scene, sugar,' she said. 'Nothing's underfoot. It's just easier if we move it.'

'Easier because the cops know where the body is?' I followed her as she headed toward her bedroom and the closet.

'You used to be so much smarter, kid,' she said, pulling out a pair of low-heel pumps. 'No one knows a goddamned thing except another heel grifter blew town. No one's going to hang black crepe for your boy, honey. When you gonna get that through your head?'

'So why do we have to–'

'I decided only we should know where the body is,' she said, sliding on the shoes. 'Now are you gonna get out of that nightgown yourself or do I have to unpeel you like a grape?'

We were in the car when I started in again. My days of flying blind were over.

179

'I told you,' I said. 'I told you Mackey was gonna put the screws in.'

'Mackey's fine,' she said, punching the cigarette lighter. She didn't usually smoke. I took this as a bad sign. 'It's Upstairs,' she continued. 'Mackey's doing a little poaching, buying up their land, building a new track to compete with Casa Mar. They think he's moving in on them. I don't want us to be Mackey's cat's-paw.'

I was surprised she told me that much. She lit the cigarette. Her hands were still. She was edgy but under control. She was doing business, cleaning up.

'I told you,' I repeated, not too wisely.

'Don't mouth me, little girl,' she said, sharply but quietly. 'Mackey served his purpose and this is just insurance. And it gives us a tip-off. If Mackey tries to parlay our situation with Upstairs, we'll know it because he'll come up empty-handed.'

It was the biggest glimpse behind the curtain she'd ever given me and it was quite an eye-opener. In the end, we were so much grease to work bigger deals, to oil the gears for setups we couldn't even see, couldn't even catch a glimmer of.

'Has Mackey got a shot? Could he–'

'No,' she replied, then sealed herself up. I

could see her face close before my eyes and I knew I'd gotten the most I could. She looked at me. 'Now let's can the big noise and get this done.'

We drove about fifteen miles out of town, her talking the whole way about how I needed to shape up, get wise, stop being such a rabbit, and get my steel back. What good was all her work if, on the first big test, I turned back into some tiddlywink? She laid it on me hard.

But I wasn't listening. I was thinking about what we were going to be doing. I was thinking about what we would be moving. I didn't want to feel that weight, didn't want to go through it all again. I'd finally started distracting myself from the blood and gristle of it, the terrifying red-on-bone pictures in my head. And now I had to sink right back into it. My lily whites would really be in it this time.

We drove up a long, windy bluff until we reached a tangle of dark trees. She stopped the car and stepped out. I thought I wouldn't be able to move. My teeth were grinding together, my whole body felt like dry wood, stiff and brittle. But I did move. There was something in me that made me move. I opened the door, felt a rush of mist collapse down my throat.

She opened the trunk and handed me a flashlight and shovel and took a pair for herself too. I didn't ask where she'd gotten them. Instead, I was eyeing a mound of wet leaves under one of the swooping trees. My beam rested on it. With the air so unsettled, the whole mound seemed to be moving, shivering.

'A long way away,' a voice, my voice, shuddered out.

'Mackey doesn't want 'em too close to home anymore,' she said, and I thought I caught a little relief in her voice, like she hadn't been so sure the body was where they'd told her it would be.

She walked over to the knot of low-hanging trees and set her flashlight down. She stopped right in front of the pile and kicked her foot straight in, sending leaves everywhere. Swinging the shovel around her like a sword, she plunged it in.

As I walked slowly, carefully toward her, I thought I could smell it already. I knew that smell. When I was little, my sister's tabby disappeared. We thought she'd run away until the musty, meaty odor started from under the porch. I remember my old man holding a washcloth to his face as he dug the thing out, my sister bawling in our bedroom. The next year, the lady down the street, the one who wore leg braces, put a bullet into her brain. She lived alone in her half of the duplex and no one knew until the stench started coming through the walls. The stench, just like now.

I was right behind her, the smell hot and close in my face. I was holding the shovel and standing behind her.

'You gonna stand there like a clothes rack or start digging?' She didn't seem to notice the smell at all. She just kept shoveling.

So I started shoveling too.

And the smell got stronger and there were blowflies and the smell was like a living thing thick in the air as we dug deeper.

It didn't take long. Mackey's boys hadn't bothered to go too deep. Seeing the first piece of the canvas there, lit by the flashlights resting on the ground, I felt my mouth go dry. I didn't dare inhale. I didn't dare look at her even as I could hear her breathing.

'Here we go,' she said, as we cleared away the last shovelfuls of wet dirt.

I looked down at the long duffel bag, so sure it would be open and I'd have to see. What would it be like to see, to see that?

I pictured him curled up in there, like a baby in the womb, curling upon himself. And I could picture the bag opening, loosening, dilating out. And then I would see him, and that careless smile. He'd still be smiling at me.

'Let's go,' I heard her say. I looked over and saw she'd already opened the trunk. She was ready. She was ready. She was so easy. It was like she was about to move sacks of jewels, like any swag. Was that how it could get? Could it get like that?

And she was tugging the bag, heaving her shoulders.

And there I was lifting it with her, my breath short, my arms straining, the wet, heavy air filling my half-open mouth, the wind lifting bits of dirt and grime into it. My whole body feeling coated with the stench, the sumpy thickness that had been covering him, all that had been slipping from him, seeping into everything that I was now ankle deep in, everything I was taking in with each foul breath. It was all Vic and it was all what we'd done and it was in my skin, my lungs, everything.

She was strong and she carried the heavier end and then we were heaving it into the trunk and it was Vic in our hands. And I thought about it as the canvas burned my fingers, as my nails dug in. It was Vic.

Oh, Vic, even you deserved better than this. Even a lousy snake like you.

She slammed the trunk shut.

'Not bad, kid,' she said, and it was that near-smile of hers. 'Halfway there.'

We drove about ten miles back towards town, stopping at a salvage yard. She navigated it with such ease I figured she'd been there a hundred times or more, weaving through the towering piles of rotting fenders and crushed car doors, twisted steering columns, rusted engines, and burned-out sleeper cars.

She pulled up beside a long stretch of oil drums stacked fat for twenty yards or more. We got out and I followed her, the headlights hitting her like a spotlight.

She was ahead of me and I was watching her walk in that swaying fishtail way of hers, the cool, precise undulations that nearly hypnotized. The walk was so easy, so measured, and those legs, even streaked with dirt, were worthy of any spotlight.

And it was like she wasn't even real, a shimmer-struck illusion, a hard flash of glamour against the creaking stacks of drums, rolling against each other, furry with rust, grimy with oil and soot, perfumed with old gasoline and singing emptily as each gust of air whistled through every rutted hole and crevice.

She, lit all through, filled with light, sparking with it ... even in her spattered pumps, even with that shovel in her ungloved hand, she was a star. And I cursed her for it. Because she was solid gold, fourteen-carat, barely burnished despite twenty years of hard molling. But beneath it, I knew, beneath that gold and stardust, she was all grit and sharp teeth gnashing, head twisting, talons out, tearing flesh, she was all open mouth, tunneling into an awful nothing.

I hated her.

And I felt closer to her than ever.

Goddamn her.

We dragged the body to the newly dug grave, shallow but wedged between the tightly packed drums and a fifteen-foot-high barbed wire fence. It didn't have to be deep. No one would find him.

In the car driving home, I looked down at my hands, cold, scraped, nails torn to red ribbons fluttering loose.

I'd had him in my hands one last time. My hands on him through thick canvas. My hands on him. Even after everything – how ashamed I was to feel this now – because even after everything I still felt my hips burning at the memory of him, what he'd done to me in that dark room. In his dark room in the middle of the night. Hands moving, making my eyelids flutter back. Feeling it now, remembering it, all I could think of was knees on hard floors and this is what sin is all about.

'You really redeemed yourself, kid boots,' she was saying as the waiter brought us our strip steaks leaking red over the plate's edge. It was nearly three A.M., but Googie's stayed open for her.

She lifted her highball glass to her mouth and took a long, snug sip. Then, leaning back in her chair, she nodded at me, which was her version of beaming with pride.

I realized she thought this whole thing had brought us together. And sure, it did. Goddammit, it did. Our hands on Vic together. Our hands in that dirt, that dirt under our nails, the wetness in the air lifting that dirt onto our skin – like some ancient ritual, like it was before anything, before words, even.

It hit me: she thought we were celebrating. Hell, maybe we were.

When we got back to her place, I took some of the Tuinal the doc had given me and slept dreamlessly for ten hours. She'd left me a note, listing my stops for that day. I was back on the circuit.

I'd made three pickups around town when I started to get the itchy feeling. At first, I thought it was my head playing tricks on me, but enough looks in the rearview told me different.

I didn't recognize the car and it was too far away for me to see the driver's face, but I knew I'd seen it before. I thought maybe it'd been idling outside the betting parlor I'd hit earlier that day, but I wasn't sure.

My first thought was Gloria put a tail on me. Well, let her. I was doing exactly what I was supposed to. She had a lot of brass after what we'd done together the night before.

But it was kind of a bum-looking Dodge Coronet, nothing one of her boys would be caught dead in.

Which is when I started thinking about the cops. It sure looked like the kind of car a cop might drive.

Then I began imagining bad scenarios again. Had we been followed the night before? Nah. If we had, they'd've just hauled us in on the spot with the dirt still on our hands, in every line of our palms.

It wasn't long before the driver of the Coronet stopped bothering to pretend. He was right behind me, close enough for a second date. I even got a look at the guy and he sure had a lawman's face, weathery and saggy with a thick edge of meanness.

It wasn't a situation that left me a lot of choices. I couldn't make any more drops or pickups with him on my tail. And I was only going to give myself more heebie-jeebies if I kept wondering what the real story was.

Still half bent on the blues I'd popped at four AM., I let myself take it casual, like she would. Then I figured what she'd do next and I did it. I drove to the far end of town, picked an empty side street, and pulled over, stopping the car. The Coronet driver stopped too.

I got out and walked to the Coronet, sauntering over to the driver's-side door.

'Can't say I'm not flattered, boss,' I said, doing my best side-of-the-mouth sneer. Wasn't that what he expected, what they all did? 'But I already got an old man.'

He looked up at me with that cop look: half bored and half ready to billy club me at the same time.

'You want to follow me to the station, smart girl?' he said, looking straight ahead. Not even looking at me, like I was so much trash on the curb.

'That's how it's gonna be, huh?'

'That's how it's gonna be.'

Turned out, the cop in the Coronet was just the delivery man. I was supposed to see a Detective Clancy. I'd never heard of him, figured he must be new.

Waiting in the common area, I let the tooies keep my edges numb and pretended this was just the boys looking for some behind-the-hand talk. Or maybe Clancy was taking the long way around to getting his name on the pad. Play it nice and easy, I told myself. Bing Crosby on a hammock.

'I don't like how this plays out,' a voice rustled in front of me, gruff but lilting.

I looked up to see Mackey's boy, tweed cap low on his forehead and dark with sweat.

'What they drug you in for?' he said, leaning down and speaking softly.

I looked up at him. 'Dancing with boys.'

He shook his head. 'You don't get it. You don't see the contraption. Honey it's all wired and you make one wrong move–' He stopped suddenly and stood up straight, head turning this way and that way like a cartoon robber looking for his getaway car.

'One wrong move?' I asked, trying to keep my voice level, trying not to let his nerves rub off on me.

He shook his head and, hands in pockets, gestured with his eyes, with a shift in his torso, toward the stairwell door.

I followed him down one floor to the morgue, its glazed green walls chilly and glistening. I'd only been down there once before and then I was only in the hallway, waiting with a beat cop while my old man ID'ed my mother, burnt half to char in the big county hospital blaze fifteen years back. They got her from dental records and the metal name tag seared into her chest.

For a long minute I was afraid he was taking me to show me Vic, somehow dug up and half rotted through on a slab. But it turned out he was just looking for a quiet place to talk.

'What'd they lasso you in for, copper penny?' he said.

'I don't know.'

191

Up close, his face looked sweaty, like he'd been dipped in castor oil. 'They're fishing. Watch your step. Watch your step.'

'I'm not worried. These chumps don't scare me.'

'I didn't spill, daisy,' he said. 'I didn't give 'em a butcher's inch.' Slipping off his cap, he wiped his brow with the back of his sleeve, licking his lips nervously. 'But there's bigger trouble out there than the Boys Blue, you know?'

My eyes twitched. Sure, I knew what he meant, or had a good idea.

'I'm talking about your lady. You get?'

I looked at him.

'You get?' he repeated. 'She's got eyes in the back of her head. Listen, angel. Listen. She's got eyes in the back of her head and everyplace else. I heard her talking to my guy. To Mr. Mackey.'

'When?' I said, cool, busying my hands with an invisible something underneath my fingernail.

'Today. She was putting it on, honey. She was putting quite a lot of ribbons on you, you see? And not the kind you like. Maybe he believes her and maybe he don't. But sounded to me like she all but fingered you as the button on your boy.'

192

'Why would she do that?' I said, squinting, trying to fight the quake he'd sent through me.

'She's making sure all her bets are covered. And if she'll play you for Isaac to my boss, who says she won't to her own? That's the way she dances. Don't you know it yet? I've been seeing her run her mirror act since I was in short pants. She knows how to keep things working for her. She always has things working for her. If something goes down she don't like, you're the lamb. Get it?'

'I hear you, but I'm not listening,' I said, flicking my fingernails tiredly. Even as I knew he was right. Even as I knew it was true, even as I knew it was the smart thing, even as it made my stomach turn for a thousand reasons including this: *I thought I was her girl. I thought I was her girl and she's ready to sell me. Would she really, push come shove, sell me?*

In a heartbeat.

Detective Clancy was just what you'd guess. A Scotch-Irish flush about him, his hands rough and red and always planted on his hips. Fluffy ledge of hair hanging over his forehead like a schoolboy's. Mean eyes, lashes long but with something cold and cunning nestled beneath them.

He looked at me like he knew me. Like he knew all about me. This I was used to. Cops came in different sizes and had different scars, but they were all wired the same. They all looked at you like you came off some B-girl assembly line, molded plastic dolls with the shine worn off from too many rough boy fingers. All you were good for was lowdown and laydowns.

The worst were the ones who didn't hold out their hands, palms up. The true believers. But Clancy didn't look like one of those. Something weary, wasted, tugged at his face. He had no fire left. Truth was, I hadn't met one of those true believers yet.

I was nervous, though, sure. Seeing the Cap down there, the things he said, the hot and desperate look in his eyes. And too, still feeling the ghostly grit of dirt under my fingernails from last night's grave robbing. If it hadn't been for the heavy dose of tooies, I'd've been shaking like a virgin bride.

'So,' Clancy said. 'Can't say you're not a familiar face to the fellas around here.'

'I support my local police department whenever I can.'

'Well, I'm pretty new around here, three weeks in, so you're going to have to show me how it is,' he said, and boy, did he think he was clever. He figured he was hustling me like the sixteen-year-old know-it-all at the local Podunk pool hall.

'How is it?' I asked, blinking my eyes like Betty Boop. Maybe he wasn't on my Dear Santa list yet, but that didn't mean he didn't want to be. And it didn't mean he wasn't on someone else's. Beneath the schoolboy peach fuzz, I could see him half on his way to turning wise, like he might not mind being wrapped in velvet. Something about the sheen on his shirt, the way his shoes squeaked. A taste he was considering letting sit on his tongue.

'You know, miss,' he said. 'The arrangement.'

'The arrangement? I'm sorry, Detective Clancy, I don't–'

'Nice try, honey,' he said, leaning back against his desk. 'Why don't you just lay it out for me. Save me some time.'

'I always like to assist the police,' I said. 'But I'm not sure how I can–'

'All right, all right,' he half groaned, rolling his eyes. 'We didn't drag you in here to talk about graft anyway, girlie. You're not here about that at all. That's small potatoes compared to what I got on you, missy.'

I fought off a flinch, put the mask on. 'Get out the hot lights,' I said, smiling with my teeth.

He hit me with Vic right away. No dinner first, no peck on the cheek. He wanted to know when the last time I saw him was. The 'Vic who?' routine didn't fly.

'We know you've been shacking up with him, so don't play the tenderfoot with me.'

'I wish I could help you, but I just don't know the fella.'

'Don't waste my time,' he said, arms folded across his chest. I didn't like his confidence. I wondered what he had. Maybe Mackey's night watchmen, the ones who'd staked out Vic's place and sold me out to Gloria, spilled to the law too. 'We have witnesses.'

'You don't have anything,' I said, twisting my legs, pretending they were a mile long like hers. 'If you did, this whole scene would be playing different. You'd be putting the hammer to me.'

'We have a witness saw you in and out of his place on more than one occasion. We have a witness who talked to Riordan himself. Riordan told this witness he'd been banging you for weeks.'

'This witness is lying to you,' I said, calm and easy. But I can't say I wasn't getting nervous.

Soon enough, he brought in a Detective Nast, another new face to me. It was like the department had changed hands overnight. And Nast, a narrow-browed, thick-jawed type, the kind who spoke without moving his lips, was no more charmed by me than Clancy and both of them were holding their cards close to their chest.

'So where'd your boyfriend go, anyway?'

'I don't have a boyfriend, Detective.'

'What happened to your face, miss?'

'What do you mean?' I asked, stopping myself before my hand rose to my cheek.

'Looks like you got knocked around recently. That a parting gift from your boyfriend, Vic?'

I wasn't sure what they knew, or if these witnesses really existed, but it was plain they knew something. And thinking of Gloria buzzing in Mackey's ear, wrapping me up for him like a Christmas package, things didn't fall right, I was starting to feel sick to my stomach.

'So how much did you steal for your boyfriend?'

'What?' I asked, and that time they could

197

probably hear the quiver just edging into my voice.

'And how come you get off scot-free and he seems to have been given a free pass to nowhere land?'

'I wish I could help you, gentlemen, but I just don't know what you're talking–'

'We have a witness who heard gunfire at Vic Riordan's apartment on the fifteenth.'

The landlady.

'And we have a witness who places you coming out of the apartment within twenty minutes of the gunfire.'

This was the bluff, I could feel it. Could feel it dripping off them, sweaty and hopeful.

'Must've been another girl,' I said. 'There's plenty like me. Aren't we a dime a dozen to you fellas?'

'And it all fits,' Clancy said. 'Because we have that witness who says Vic told her all about you.'

Her. The witness was a her.

'That Vic told her he was playing you like a ukulele and the payoff would be huge. But it was a big risk. And he liked risks, didn't he?'

'I wouldn't know.'

'Big risk because you were working with

198

him to get a big score. But you were doing it on the sly from your big boss.'

Who was this goddamned rat?

'What boss?' I replied. 'I don't have a boss. I'm between jobs.'

'Your boss Gloria Denton. Gloria Denton, the lady, the legend,' Clancy said, his teeth shiny, like he was practicing his front-page face already.

There it was. I saw the whole deal now. They wanted her. They wanted her.

'I don't know–'

'You can't play that game in this building, little miss,' Nast said, running a toothpick back and forth along his gums. 'Everyone here knows about you and the pad. The ones on it aren't talking. That's how we know who's on it.'

'And that's why you got sent here, huh? To clean up the joint?' I smirked. 'Best of luck.'

'Oh that ain't all,' Clancy said, smirking back at me. 'We know Riordan's dead as mutton. We know it. And you're going to tell us how it happened.'

'I don't know a goddamned thing,' I said, leaning back in my chair and swinging one leg over the other. 'But I got time if you do.'

They danced me for two, three hours. I

didn't dip for them, didn't do any twirls. I never once pressed my chest close, even to tease. I wouldn't be singing in their ear. Even with the feeling maybe I still had about Vic, *Vic trapped in that bag, pressed against hard prongs of barbed wire, all that gaudy energy choked under seeping oil drums, all alone, all alone,* even with the Mackey ruckus, with what she'd done, was doing, could do, I didn't see ever giving it up to these meter maids. What would be the dividend? Keep me from behind crossbars? Maybe, if I thought they could hang it on me. But if they really had something on me, they'd've shown it by now.

That's what I told myself at least.

'Let's take a breather,' Clancy said, looking over at Nast meaningfully. 'Give her some time to think things over.'

They walked me into a room down the hall, parked me in a metal chair, gave me nothing but a wall to stare at. My palms were wet, I admit it. But as nervous as I might be, they could never touch the scares she could put in me. All this seemed like hopscotch compared to one dark look from her.

I was in the room for five minutes when the door opened and a heady gust of tuberose rushed me in the face.

'I told them I'd squawk,' a voice needled through me, 'but only if I got to tell you what a no-good tramp you are when they pulled you in.'

I looked up.

The furrier.

Twitchy little Regina, the rotten bitch. Risen from rumored death or Siberia. To play the rat.

'What'd I ever do to you?' I asked, rising to my feet.

Fluffing out her poodle collar and shaking her springy curls, she shot a hard look. 'How about making a play for my boyfriend while I'm on the lam for him, ducking his lousy collectors?' She puffed out her chest and walked right up to me. It was quite a show. 'You may play class, but you're all whore,' she continued, jabbing her thumb at her breast. 'Vic's my man.'

I put on a big grin. 'Yeah, well, he never mentioned that when he was fucking me.'

She winced, but then came right back at me. 'Probably too busy biting his knuckle, trying not to get sick,' she said, trying to regain her bluster, swinging her mink-tipped wrap around her like the queen of the station house.

I felt my temples pulse. 'You think you can put the frame on me, shaver,' I said, my voice hard and unfamiliar. 'Just you try. I'll have you in pieces on the floor. Three cracks and–' I snapped my fingers in her face like I was Little Caesar. It was quite a show.

Inside, though, I tried to get my head working. What had Vic told her? What had she told the cops? Always keep in front, that's what I'd been taught. Don't get stuck in the heat. Move to the cool space three beats ahead.

'You don't scare me,' she said, tossing her mink muff purse down and resting her palms flat on the tabletop like cops in the movies. 'You're just an errand boy. I know all about you.'

I gave her a stare with a slight smile and didn't say a word. She was so high on nerves I figured it would throw her. It did. I could see it in the way her body clenched up, her jaw went tight, lashes flapping. Worked better than all the brassy talk. I kept the stare going until she broke it.

'I told the badges all about you,' she said, fighting a tremble in her voice. 'Vic used to telephone me. He used to telephone me and say how he was putting it to you and if he put it to you long enough, he'd be in clover. We both would.'

'Let me guess,' I said calmly, working like I knew she would, like I knew Gloria would. 'You heard whispers that he was seeing me and you called him, threatened to squeal, to throw him to his sharks. So then he says, "No, Regina, it ain't that way. I'm doing it for you, for us." Was that how it was, Regina?'

The mink paws around her shoulders began to quake, tiny claws clicking against their beady glass eyes. Her eyelashes fluttered.

'He promises you, like he's promised you a million times,' I went on. '"Just one last score, baby, so we can be together."' I stretched my voice out like Vic's. I looked Regina in the eye and gave her my best crooked Vic smile. '"I'd like to deck you out in diamonds, baby. You deserve more than late-night rolls with me after some other gee's bought you dinner. I'd like to have you on my arm at the tony joints, swing you round the dance floor, take you to a show every night, bring you home and lay you down on satin sheets and look at you knowing I had something in my pocket more than a last-chance chip. Isn't that what you want, baby.'"

As my mouth wrapped around his honeyed words, I could see it hitting her hard, knocking all the air out of her. Her face lost its color, began to look small, like the softly shaking head of a half-broken doll.

'What'd you do to Vic?' she said, her voice just a quiver.

There it was. He had her on the love rack. I could see it on her, could see everything he'd done to her, how he'd gotten under her skin. More than that. I could see her.

I wondered what my face looked like to her. What she could see on me.

'I didn't do anything to Vic,' I said. 'Not a thing, baby.'

'Where is he?' she asked, sinking down into the metal folding chair. She looked up at me, big eyes brimmed over. 'Is he finis?'

'I don't know, kid,' I said. 'But you're making things a lot more dangerous for him by saddling up for these yokels.'

She nodded, almost to herself. For a moment I was ready for waterworks. But she just looked back up at me, blinking.

'He broke me,' she said and I knew it was truer even than she meant.

I gave her a hard sell, even though she didn't need it. Told her to clam up, that the more heat they put on it, the more likely Vic was to stay lost and was that what she wanted, really? Or worse still, guffing all over town might put the spotlight on him, leading the sharks straight to him. Then it really would be finis.

By the time I was done I'd half convinced myself Vic could still be saved.

She fell hard, like I knew she would, and by the time Clancy and Nast returned, she was recanting like Galileo. Grim-faced, they tossed me out of the station house, but first they gave me a good earful about how they knew all about me and all about my boss. They didn't have what they needed on me now, but they were sure it was only a matter of time.

'Don't even think about beating town,' Clancy said, hands on me like I was some pink pants on the boulevard. 'And if you've got anything rattling around up there under all that hair, you'll be back within twenty-four hours to sing for us. 'Cause if we make a case without you, you'll be riding the lightning seat along with your boss come springtime.'

I gave him a blank face. I didn't even know what he was talking about.

Sure, I left feeling like I'd won something big, slid out from some clutches, but that feeling was long gone by the time I'd driven back to her place, our place. I'd beaten one rap, for the time being, but I was headed back into a different kind of stir.

Taking the elevator up, my stomach twisted at the thought of seeing her again, the first time since our little excavation party. And that sent me back to thinking of Vic, of Vic in pieces, of the sweet tang of rotting oil drums, the raw smell of pooling sewage. And that sent me to thinking of her again, the way she'd been, the way she could be again. Would this go on forever?

'Where've you been?' She looked ready to go out, dressed in a long, jade-colored suit, an eel-skin bag in her hand. 'I got calls you were hours late for half your drops.'

'I thought I was being followed,' I said carefully.

'Followed? By who?' And the way she said it was like she wasn't worried for a second that I might have really been tailed. I got it fast: she was worried that I might be so loaded up on nerves that I might think I was.

'I don't know,' I said. 'I shook whoever it was. Maybe it was nobody.'

She had her eyes on me, doing that thing, reading me, reading my worth. Was I too far gone to risk keeping around? Was I more trouble than I was worth?

'What kind of car?'

'A Chrysler Imperial, hardtop,' I lied, tugging off my suit jacket. 'Listen, I'm okay now. I was shaky, but it's past. I've got it together. I've got it beat.'

'Okay,' she said, still watching me. 'I'm going up to Tunsdell and won't be back until tomorrow morning. I need you to drive me to the train station.' She looked me up and down. 'But first, beef Wellington at Hy's. You look like you need something in your mouth.'

I nodded and walked by her, headed toward the bathroom. As I did, I glanced over into her bedroom. The closet door was open and, in that fleeting instant, I could see something trailing out. And I knew what it was. A beaded evening coat, peacock green.

I walked into the bathroom and shut the door. I knew several things at once and all of them were making my mouth go dry, my blood sing. That coat had been hanging at the very back of the closet. That coat was only worn in the winter. That coat only could have been pulled aside for one reason. For the thing hidden behind it. My dress. She was looking for my dress. The dress I'd worn that night. The dress I'd burned to soft ash in the basement incinerator. She knew I knew. She knew and who could guess what she'd do.

'When are you going to show your hand, Gloria?'

My voice thick with Manhattans, I felt the words coming from my mouth, I couldn't stop them. Since we'd sat down at Hy's Steakhouse, I'd been knocking back the drinks, trying to stop my hands from shaking, trying to fight off the dread.

But the booze both jazzed up the panic and gave me some nerve. Wasn't that what booze was for? Wasn't that why she never needed it? I leaned my elbow forward, nearly sliding it into the half-empty dinner plate in front of me. I felt like there were no rules left. Why not say anything? That was how I felt. What was left to lose? Beating that furrier at her own game so handily, ending it with my heel on her chicken neck had really worked me up, fixed me with some kind of crazy courage.

'When are you going to show me your hand?' I heard my voice repeat itself. 'How long are you going to make me wait?'

'You really shouldn't drink, kid,' she said, uncapping her lipstick. But something in her tone told me she knew what I was talking about.

'You'd sell me for a sawbuck,' I said, my head wobbling. 'What're you waiting for? My next slipup?'

'That what you think?' she asked.

'I don't think it,' I said, hoisting my shoulders, almost not believing I'd made it this far, said this much. Don't think I didn't get the joke of it all: I was pulling it off only because I was aping her. 'I don't think it,' I repeated. 'I know it. I saw the dress in your closet. My dress from that night. You were holding it. You figured me for a patsy. Just like Vic did. Well, I'm no patsy.'

'No?' she said, raising an eyebrow. I thought I saw a flicker of amusement in her eyes and it made me madder.

'No,' I said roughly. 'I'm no one's goddamned pigeon. I burned it, Gloria. I burned the dress all up. So good luck. I got rid of it and it's gone and you've got nothing on me. I beat you out of the gate.'

'I know you got rid of it,' she said, running a slash of crimson across her face, across the faintest lines above her upper lip.

'I figured that too,' I said, trying for a smirk. 'I saw the closet open tonight. See, I beat you to it, Gloria. I did.'

'Sure I knew you got rid of it, cream puff,' she said, popping open that tortoiseshell compact of hers and appraising her handiwork. 'I'd've been pretty disappointed if you hadn't. I hope I've done a better job on you than that.'

I felt the warm alcohol swirl away and my chest grow frigid, all in an instant. 'You meant for me to find it,' I said, realizing it as I said it.

'I had to know you had your head on straight, kid. Lately, you've had a pretty shaky trigger finger. Soft-headed moves, phantom tail jobs.'

'No,' I said, shaking my head. 'You were holding it. You were holding it as insurance.'

'Insurance against what? What do you think I could be scared of? Nothing you could throw my way, junior.' She capped the lipstick and dropped it into her purse. 'Listen, if you tangled with me, I wouldn't toss you to the bulls.'

'Mackey,' I blurted out. 'How about to Mackey?'

'Or Mackey either,' she said without skipping a beat. 'I may throw a few distractions his way, a bluff or two to keep him guessing. But that's beside the point. If I found out you really tangled with me, kid,' she said, fixing me in the eye, 'I think you know what I'd do. I take care of my own business. Right?'

'Right,' I said, without thinking. I didn't need to think. There was nothing to think about.

I can say it. She'd put a fear in me. I couldn't let go of it. I couldn't see how it would ever stop. We were chained together, cuffed at the wrist, the ankle, the hip. What would the escape be? There was no end, far as I could see, Well, one. My throat open like a long pink seam. Or hers. But I didn't have her steel. I knew that. So it'd be me.

I had to sell her. What choice did I have?

I'd done it once. She was the sap for thinking I wouldn't do it again.

'I'm yours, Clancy.'

I called from the pay phone at the rail station, dialing the minute her train slipped from view.

The words were out and I felt it all falling apart around me. I felt it all breaking up inside me.

'You're doing the right thing,' he said in his cop voice. And part of me wanted to smash his face in. But part of me thought at least I had this going for me. As rotten as I felt, it was what my old man might've called the standup thing to do, right? Maybe that mattered to someone, somewhere. Maybe somewhere in me that mattered.

But then I thought, what did the old man know, really? Still making beans after thirty years on the job. Getting pushed around by a bunch of bohunks. Sitting in the back of the church on Sunday getting yelled at by the priest about what lousy sinners we all were. Getting the fish eye from the bank whenever he's a day late on payments he's been making regular, nails to bone, for two decades or more. Oh, Pop...

But if I wanted to lay it all out there, lay it bare, there was this: Look at how she sold me short. Look at how she thought I was all hers and not strong enough to take her. Turns out maybe I could take her, take her and still come out clean and all by my own rules and there was nothing she could do.

I was still half lit from the Manhattans on the way to the junkyard. It was better that way because it put a hazy mist around all the corners, made it all seem part of the same long nightmare. The kind where you keep ending up in the same place no matter how far you try to go. You're in deepest Africa, the Casbah, Red China, and the Pyramids, and then somehow you're back in your own bed, coverlet to chin.

The salvage yard was just as damp and foggy as the night before, the smell just as earthy and sickly sweet. Clancy had to swerve for a pair of mean-faced raccoons, nearly hitting the end of a long row of steel canisters.

'Your kind of joint, eh?' he said as our feet sunk into the spongy ground.

'You're getting what you want,' I said, my tongue still heavy, my words slow.

I led the way, my ankles spattered, itching, eyes on the barbed wire fence, ears filled with that moaning wind through the metal skeletons, the empty drums.

'Over there,' I said. 'This is as close as I'm getting.'

Clancy and Nast trudged toward the

fence. I leaned up against a sleeper car and pulled out a cigarette, nearly lighting before a strong waft of gasoline knocked me in the face and I thought better of it.

I was waiting for the bad feeling to come back when I saw that canvas bag. I was trying not to think about what might happen when they found it. When they opened it. When they opened it and I would have to see, even from a distance.

But when I looked over, the detectives were just standing there alongside the family rocking drums. At first they'd poked their heads around, even rolling some of the drums this way and that. But now they were just standing there.

Finally, Clancy beckoned me with his arm. As I tramped over, though, I got it. I got it and here I was all over again. I got it hard, a haymaker right to the gut.

The body was gone.

They had me under the hot lights for real this time.

My head a jumbled mess, I spilled but good. They believed me, sure. They believed that Gloria Denton had given Vic Riordan a one-way ticket to Golden Slumbers. They believed she'd buried him, or had him buried. They believed all that. But what good did it do?

They had nothing to hang their hat on, not even a body. And what use was the word of a piece like me? A B-girl, a B-boy runner, a girl with a lifetime of mug shots and States-ville stints and world-class beatings from hard-fisted boys ahead of her and who-knew-what behind her.

I didn't want to do it.

But now I had even less of a choice.

I didn't want to do it because I still felt ripped up inside.

I didn't want to do it because I still didn't like laying it open for the blue.

I didn't want to do it because it was my last stake and I didn't want to give it up unless I had to.

But I had to.

'I have the gun,' I said, finally. 'I have the gun and the blade. I took them and I hid them. I have them both,' I said, so I couldn't take it back.

The die was thrown, so loud you could hear it thump on the green felt.

Fuck me, Gloria, I had to play you this

way. I did.

They drove me to my apartment. Walking through it, with the blinds down and more than a week's worth of dust gathering on the chrome, the glass, I felt like a trespasser, a burglar. Like it had never really been mine. Which, truth told, it hadn't.

I led them to the bedroom closet. They stood there and watched as I pulled the hatbox down from the uppermost shelf and removed the lid for them.

My hands weren't even shaking as I lifted the mohair cloche hat from the layers of tissue paper and flipped it over so they could see the revolver, its gold grips glinting, and the burnished letter opener, tacky with old blood.

Looking at them now, they didn't even seem real. They seemed like so many glittering trinkets that had glided through my gloved hands, the endless stream of bright-colored swag I'd passed from hard boy to tough guy to hard boy without ever letting it touch my skin.

Clancy paused for a second, then looked over at Nast, who was bouncing on the balls of his feet. Both of them started beaming like it was a goddamned birthday cake just for them.

I didn't tell you about keeping the gun, the letter opener. I wasn't sure I would ever use them. I didn't tell you. I didn't like to think about keeping them, holding them. Or about tossing the knife I'd used on Vic's hand, long ago tossing it down a sewer drain. I didn't think about any of it if I could help it. Didn't like how it made me come off. Like I was a double-crosser, a fink, a Judas every chance I got. It wasn't that way. She'd taught me. I was doing what she'd taught me, what any kid at the head of the class would do. No matter what you see, do, are a part of, no matter how hot, crazy, out of control things get, you gotta be thinking three steps ahead. How can I make this play right for me? Save yourself, serve yourself. She taught me that. That's what I'm saying. I'm saying it was her.

'You're the candy kid,' Clancy was telling me, back at the station house, nearing seven A.M.
'My prints are on it too,' I said. 'Don't think about selling me. I played it square.'
He smiled. 'You can unfurrow, sweetheart.'
'You don't interest us at all,' Nast said,

217

sliding me a cup of gray coffee.

'It'll be over soon,' Clancy added, like he was my kindly uncle now that I'd given it up for him.

'Why do I have to be there?' I said, twisting in my skirt, numb as a housewife on Saturday night.

'We're not taking any chances,' Clancy said, shoving a bear claw into his mouth. 'Not with this one. She trusts you and we gotta use that.'

'You pick her up at the train station like regular,' Nast said, straightening his holster. 'We're watching nearby.'

'She can spot a tail a mile–'

'We'll be a good distance,' Clancy said, mouth still glistening with pastry glaze. 'We'll follow you back to her place and make the cuff. Easy as apple pie. You just gotta stand back and watch the show.'

It was all happening so fast I didn't have time to look at the thing. Before I knew it, I was sitting at the wheel at the deserted station, watching her walk toward the car.

That was when it started to hit me and I felt my leg go jerky, start shaking, my heel rattling against the gas pedal.

It was looking at her, looking at her

coming through the early morning mist, head high, auburn hair swept up off her face, those enormous white-framed sunglasses, her fitted suit in creamy seafoam, those endless legs winding and unwinding with each step, her whole body arching and snapping like the showgirl she was.

I want the legs, that's what I thought.

Walking toward me like that, she seemed ageless. Eternal. She could be one or a thousand years old and always be like this, always be walking slowly toward me, eyes on me, knowing everything. Giving me everything.

She gave me everything.

But it was too late thinking like that now. The time had passed for shimmery regrets like some kind of ladies' picture tugging tears at the Bijou. We were never meant for that.

Her hand on the door, the filmy air flush on my face as she opened it...

'You look like you slept with your face mashed into a carpet,' she said, as she settled herself in the seat. 'Don't tell me you picked yourself up a new toy last night.'

I didn't say anything, but my leg stopped shaking and I hit the gas.

As we drove the three miles to her place, she was yapping the whole way. About the mess she had to clean up in Tunsdell, about how everything had gotten jammed up when I was down for the count and now she had to work twice as hard to get the operation running again. You couldn't leave any one of those stooges and filchers alone for a day without them mucking things up, one of them beating some sad-sack delivery man into a coma over a busted case of gin, another skimming off last night's winnings, then blowing the wad at the carpet joint next door, one forcing himself on a cigarette girl, and another knocking around some coffee shop waitress until she cried bloody murder. It never ended. It just showed how you had to keep on top of everything all the time. No more slipups like the kind that had put us in this hole. We had to keep things running smooth as country cream or we were in for more trouble.

'I'm sorry,' I said, trying not to glance in the rearview mirror. Trying not to see if Clancy and Nast were in sight. 'It won't happen again.' I kept my eyes on the road.

She didn't say anything, but I could tell she was looking at me.

'I don't mean to lay it all on you, kid,' she

said, which surprised me. 'It's just a bump in the road.'

I nodded, feeling something vaguely pinching, tickling in my chest. I know it might not seem like much, but I'd never heard her say anything like that.

'Before you came along,' she went on, 'I had to do it all myself and no one even to spill to.'

I felt my eyes turning hot. Goddamn her.

I couldn't talk in the elevator up to her place and I knew it looked fishy. But I thought if I talked, my voice would do things, that I wouldn't be able to stop it from shaking or going queer on me. I had a hard time looking her in the face too.

Standing there, I fixed my eyes on her hands, her white netted gloves. I made myself think about what those hands had done, could do. I thought about those hands wrapped around a brass blade, curled around gold grips. I thought about her face, what it could become, what she had shown me. The thing she had shown me, it would never leave. It was a scar just as thick and sealed over as those burn marks the bosses put on her. She had no right to leave those marks on me, bound as we were.

'You should clean up,' she said as she unlocked the door and we stepped in. 'You go around looking like that, people are gonna think you spent the night tossing at a sawdust joint.'

'Okay,' I said, heart battering around in my chest. Would they come right away? Was it going to happen now? If they didn't come now, could I hold on?

She set her overnight satchel on top of the tall console against the wall and opened it.

'I have something,' she said.

'A delivery for me?'

'No.' She pulled out a small bag of cream-colored velvet. 'Something for you.'

I fidgeted, wrenching off one of my gloves and twisting it with the other hand. Was she going to pull this now? Was she going to give me a present right before I knifed her for the bulls?

She handed me the bag. She couldn't help but see my hands trembling as I took it.

'It's not a diamond necklace, kid,' she said. 'Don't get rattled.'

I shook the bag over my open hand and out dropped a long, narrow object, heavy for its size.

I stifled a gasp. It was a letter opener. Instead of the two heads at the top it was one woman's head, with flowing hair that wrapped around the bronze blade, stem to sharp tip. Other than that, it was the same, felt the same. And the feeling of it in my hand was terrible. *Vic's chest, the sound in his throat, the way his eyes had fallen back, struck.*

'It's not exactly like before,' she said. 'But it's close.'

'Why ... why would you give me this?' I felt my head go light. My hand to my chest, I began to think I might faint, like some girl.

'What do you mean?' she said, raising an eyebrow. 'It's a replacement.'

'Why would you want to remind me of that? Of what you did to him?'

She shook her head. She even seemed to turn a little pale with surprise. 'It ain't like that, kid. Don't you get it? That gift, it was the only thing anyone ever gave me. You see? It was the only thing I ever got like that.'

Her voice, as she said it, was steely as ever, but the soft words, they were rough on me. They did things to me. Even as I held that horrible thing in my hand, the words felt like knives in my ears.

At the same time, though, it hit me even harder how much all of this had to end. How much it had to be over. If I waited any longer, I might stop seeing that. Then it would be me and her, her and me, forever.

'Don't you get it, Gloria?' I said, dropping the letter opener on the table. 'I thought you'd get it by now.'

Before I could go on, not even sure what I was going to lay on her, the doorbell rang. Shaking off her heavy gaze, her slightly surprised eyes, I went to answer it. It was Clancy and Nast, guns out.

I whipped around to see her face. I wanted to see her face when it happened. Even as I thought it might really turn me to stone.

But her face showed nothing. It was the same arch mask. Smooth, expressionless, like a mannequin, a picture in a magazine, glossy and flat and untouchable.

'Don't move,' Clancy was saying. 'Hands in the air.'

'Which one is it,' she was saying in that granite voice of hers. 'Make up your mind.'

'Get those goddamned hands in the air, Miss Denton,' Nast said, moving in on her.

She looked over at me. She looked at me to see what part I was playing – innocent bystander, accomplice, or worse.

But she could see the way it was going, the way they weren't even looking at me. And I wasn't trying to pretend. I didn't bother to pretend.

It's true. I wanted her to see. I wanted her to see I'd sung. I wanted her to see I'd sold her even as she'd given me everything and was ready to give me more.

I watched her eyes as she ran the numbers, jerked the lever, figured the odds, and it came up me. The look in her eyes when she realized there was no other way to figure it, when she knew I was the finger man and this was it – the look was nothing I'd ever seen in her before. It wasn't the cold, snaky wrath, it wasn't the frenzied, red fury. It was something sad, pulsing, unshut.

It was there in her face, open and bare, for an instant

But then it disappeared like a face card flipping over. And the hard face returned. And she had her hand on her overnight satchel.

And Clancy and Nast were moving in and shouting.

And I thought she might go for a gun.

She looked like she might.

'For that lousy chalk player?' she was saying to me. 'You fingered me for some two-bit hustler with a head of hair and some shiny teeth?'

'You shouldn't have done it,' I found myself shouting. 'Why'd you have to break him like that, Gloria?' Even as I knew Vic was just one of my reasons for selling her like I did. There were so many. It was the easiest reason to give.

'You should've thanked me,' she snarled.

And I saw her go for the letter opener.

I saw her go for it and then I knew what she was going to do. I knew it and I couldn't move and the cops were shouting their heads off because they didn't see what she was going to do. But I did. I did.

She had her eyes on me the whole time she lifted its blade. Her eyes on me, dark and bottomless, as she dug its sharp tip fast, hard, and deep into her throat. She knew just how and where and she did it and–

Her face. Her face.

They got halfway across the room before it was over. They caught her before she hit the floor but her throat was already open, the blood pirouetting.

They were holding on to her, surrounding her, and when I walked over, I saw Clancy's hands clasped tight around the frothing wound, red sluicing from between his fingers, Nast on his radio, voice high and frantic.

I looked down at them, looked down and caught her face, whiter than white, eyes staring up. They were still looking at me. Maybe they'd always be looking at me.

Clancy said he'd never have believed it if he hadn't seen it himself.

'If I hadn't been standing right there, I would've called it homicide. Never saw anyone do that to their own throat like that, straight to the artery,' he said, shaking his head grimly. 'The white coats say it's impossible. But I saw it.'

Nast nodded, his face a little green. We were back at the station house.

'What a waste,' Clancy said. 'We weren't going after her. We were going to use her to get to the big boys.'

'She wouldn't have gone for that,' I said, surprised to hear my own voice, low and calm. 'She wouldn't play the stool for you.'

'Bet she thought the same of you,' he said.

'No,' I said, taking my gloves out of my purse and putting them on. 'You don't get it.'

I looked down at my hands, stretched out my fingers. I felt like I could see things now I'd never seen before.

'She was so much better than me,' I said, as if to myself.

Clancy paused, then said, 'But look.'

'Yeah,' I said, getting up to go.

They never found Vic's body. In some ways, I was glad, though I couldn't say why. Somehow it fit Vic that he wouldn't be in any fixed place, at least not for long. Now instead of in some junkyard or on some slab, I would forever be able to picture him on the move, flashing smile, bounding forward, eyes always on the horizon, on the next shot, the next roll, the flip of another card, the next chance to lose it all, all over again.

I gave Clancy and Nast some information, some drop spots, some clip joint addresses. They knew most of it anyway. I didn't have that much to give. I was on the outside. I never got inside. She'd been careful that way and now it paid off. But I knew they'd keep me in their sights, in case. They told me not to leave town, but I knew damn sure I couldn't stick around.

I was probably safe, sure. No one knew I was a rat. No one but the furrier and she was a rat too. No one knew my real name to find me. I could just slip away.

I thought about going back to the old man, showing him how I might have taken a wrong turn back there but in the end I'd fixed things and maybe that somehow made up for a year or more of making bucks off the sins both venial and mortal of lost souls and indulging in many of those same sins myself. He'd glower and sulk and send me to confession and make me have long meetings with Father Bernard, but I'd come out okay and start things fresh, clean hands, clear eyes, a still dewy-faced girl ready to make some clean-shaven, honest working stiff, probably some lunch-bucket worker from the neighborhood, a good home, a decent home, a home with laughing children and a crucifix on the wall above the bed.

In the end, though, I got in the Impala – *my* Impala now – and drove thirteen miles downriver, stopping in the first town I'd never been to that I knew wasn't one of ours. Theirs. Hers. It looked just big enough to get lost in and just small enough that there was no action. Friday night poker games on lazy cul-de-sacs seemed as lively as it got and that was okay by me.

I had a small stack of cash I'd grabbed from my apartment before I beat town, a few pieces of paste I could pawn in a pinch, but, not enough to high-life it on for more than a banker's holiday. Two weeks in, I was doing payroll at Lavery's Department Store, a big brick eyesore that ruled the main thoroughfare and looked straight off the curled pages of the Currier and Ives calendar on the kitchen wall when I was a kid.

There I was, back punching numbers at a metal desk, back in sensible flats and high-neck blouses, the stuff office girls wear in towns like this one, and back making a lousy dime. At least I wasn't taking the bus.

A few weeks on the job, I caught the women's wear manager giving me some long looks while I was straightening my seams in the employee lounge. But it turned out she just wanted to tell me if I went down to the beauty parlor on the first floor for a Madame Rose Hair Color Bath in Champagne Blonde or Moon Gold, then she could use me as a showroom model for the mainliners and flush out-of-towners. And of course there was some off-the-books coin to be had if you played it right. I told her I'd think about it.

Not two days later, the office manager told me to skip the drugstore lunch counter and go to Gould's Restaurant at twelve sharp instead.

'What's the idea?'

'The boss – the owner – wants to meet you.'

'Mr. Lavery?'

'There is no Mr. Lavery. Not since he took a dive out the housewares window in 'twenty-nine. I mean the moneybags who owns the operation now.'

'Why does he want to be bothered with me?'

'I can think of a few ideas,' he said wearily. He looked like he felt a little sorry for me and I pictured myself spending my future days running around some big shot's desk like out of a Sunday paper cartoon.

Gould's at noontime was packed with every red-faced banker and merchant on Main Street. It was one of those brass-rail, mahogany-bar, steak-and-spinach places that midsized towns everywhere have, where all the bosses tucked into their white-napkin and martini lunches while all their employees were stuck belly to some drugstore lunch counter for ham sandwiches five days a week.

'Follow me, miss,' the maitre d' said.

I had a pretty good idea what to expect, but I figured at least I'd get a New York strip out of it.

Feeling like a bump-and-grinder walking

into a smoker, I tucked my purse under my arm, adjusted my skirt, and made my way through the smoky throng.

At first, I thought I was seeing things when I passed by the far end of the bar and spotted a familiar man leaning on the mahogany, talking to the bow-tied bartender.

And then I saw I wasn't.

Amos Mackey.

What was he doing here?

What was he doing in this Sunday school, church social, Fourth of July picnic kind of town?

For a split second, I thought maybe he was coming after me.

That he was coming after me for who knew what but at the very least for squealing to the cops.

But it didn't look that way.

And he had no reason to come after me himself when he had plenty of musclemen to do it for him.

As I passed, I could see, out of the corner of my eye, that he'd spotted me. And as I kept walking, I could feel his eyes on me and it wasn't like he was figuring an angle. No. No. Something in the way he fastened his eyes on me, it was like he had something for me.

But here's the thing: I couldn't believe the fast jolt it gave me. He wasn't the type to set me going, but there was something. Something in the way he stood there, like a king, manicured hand curling around the edge of the bar like it was the arm of his throne, watching everything, appraising.

And knowing something about me, knowing it.

Who could guess, really, how much he might know about me.

So sure, I gave him my best walk, half class, half pay-broad. If you can twist those two tightly, fellas don't know what hit 'em. They can't peg you. It gets them – the smart ones – going. Spinning hard trying to fix you. You're like the best parts of their grammar school sweetheart and their first whore all in one sizzling package.

The maitre d' ushered me to a corner table, empty except for a half-full highball glass with a twist. That was when I got the picture. Even if it hit me too late to run the odds or figure out how to play it. Within a few seconds, Mackey had seated himself across from me in front of the highball and the waiter in the starched uniform was setting another one in front of me.

Mackey looked at me, eyes slightly

hooded, gold watch fob knocking light into my eyes. He was smiling slightly, mouth closed, and he was rapping his round, baby pink fingers on the white tablecloth.

'Do the new hires down in stock rate this kind of treatment too, boss?' I said, pulling off my gloves finger by finger.

'I've been looking for you for a while,' he said quietly.

Then, folding his hands together on the table, he told me how his boys had been heeling for me for a few weeks, finally tracked me down through the Impala. And he'd been staking out this turf anyway, looking for virgin snow.

'I made Lavery's an offer and bought the whole operation for a song,' he said, bright white collar nudging against the smooth skin of his jaw. 'So here I am your employer.'

Listening to him, staring at the untouched drink in front of me, I figured maybe he didn't just want me to shimmy for my supper after all. Maybe he wanted me to cook his books for him. So I asked if that was what he had in mind.

He almost laughed, said that wasn't so. He wouldn't waste my time on that. Looking me in the eye but still leaning back in his chair, arms relaxed, head slightly tilted, he said he had big, big plans for me.

It was like this: he was moving in on my old bosses. They were going the way of the pantaloon and waxed mustache, he said. And then he fixed me with his eyes and they became darker, more purposeful. In spite of myself, I felt he was passing along a great secret to me and I'd better listen up.

'I'm the future, kid,' be said, with a kind of serene force. 'I'm the next four decades.'

He said it and it was as though a long, long war had finally ended, after many battles waged and blood drawn, and now the rightful victor had been crowned with laurels on his head, spoils at his feet, and all enemies vanquished. He said it and you knew with your gut it was true, or true enough.

'Congratulations,' I said, still not touching my drink. 'What's it got to do with me?'

His smile grew just slightly. I could smell the Sen-Sen on his breath, the expensive hair tonic. His silk shirt rustled ever so faintly against his suit jacket as he leaned forward, just a few inches.

'I want you to work for me. And not in payroll.'

I felt that jolt again, harder this time. But I kept it cool. 'Work for you like breaking in your featherbed?'

He shook his head, again with that smile that didn't show his teeth. It was the smile of a man who hadn't been surprised in a very long time but who felt like he was finally going to be surprised again and was enjoying it.

I wondered if he knew I'd stooled for the cops. I wondered if he still believed, had ever believed whatever Gloria whispered in his ear about me, about what I had done or could do. Then I figured he might know but not care. Then I figured he might know and think that it showed something in me, hard and smart and ruthless and striving, that he could use.

'It's like this,' he said, spreading his palms on the table. And he laid it out. I'd be his girl. I'd do the pickups, drop-offs, the pad. I'd handle the casinos, the tracks, big and small, the grind joints, the high-hat restaurants, the after-hours loading docks, and everything in between.

Everything would pass through my hands before it would touch his.

'Consider it ... a promotion,' he said, and I thought maybe he winked as he said it, but it might have been the light off his diamond stickpin.

I told him I needed time to think on it, to walk it around the park a little. He said fine and ordered us two porterhouse specials.

When mine was set before me, so rare it was matching me pulse for pulse, I stared at it like it was a hypnotist's spiral.

It was there and I knew it. I knew what I was good for. I knew the payoff and the price.

My hands on everything, like resting on a pile of jewels, pressing my palms into the sharp angles, pressing them hard enough to break skin. There would be endless diamonds, slithery jade cuffs, pearls like drops of custard, the glittery crust of filigreed brooches, slick topaz bracelets too heavy for me to lift my wrist. There'd be the thunder, the nervy thrills of the track, torn tickets fluttering through the air, collecting like leaves under my feet, my teetering moll heels. Better still, the hazy, sex-tipped groan of the casinos, everyone working, sweating, toiling for the payoff the big hit. I could listen to the soft rake across the felt, the rubbing of chips between eager fingers, the gallop of the roulette ball, the whispers, sighs, trembles shuddering through the whole sin-heady joint. I could listen to all of it forever.

Say good-bye to all that? Who did I think I was fooling? I was made for it, built for it,

dipped in flashy gold and ready for pluck-
ing.

I wanted more.

'I'm your girl,' I said.

The publishers hope that this book has given you enjoyable reading. Large Print Books are especially designed to be as easy to see and hold as possible. If you wish a complete list of our books please ask at your local library or write directly to:

Magna Large Print Books
Magna House, Long Preston,
Skipton, North Yorkshire.
BD23 4ND

This Large Print Book, for people
who cannot read normal print,
is published under the auspices of

THE ULVERSCROFT FOUNDATION

... we hope you have enjoyed this book.
Please think for a moment about those
who have worse eyesight than you ...
and are unable to even read or enjoy
Large Print without great difficulty.

You can help them by sending a
donation, large or small, to:

**The Ulverscroft Foundation,
1, The Green, Bradgate Road,
Anstey, Leicestershire, LE7 7FU,
England.**
or request a copy of our brochure for
more details.

The Foundation will use all donations
to assist those people who are visually
impaired and need special attention
with medical research, diagnosis
and treatment.

Thank you very much for your help.